Puffin Books
Editor: Kaye Webb

Jennifer, Hecate, Macbeth, and me

'I've decided to make you an apprentice witch,' said Jennifer. And we headed for Samellson Park, where Jennifer laid a magic circle. 'Watch me,' she said. 'When I'm ready, I'll point to you. When I point to you, you may enter the magic circle. But be quiet. Don't sneeze, burp, or breathe loud. Also, don't talk.'

Then Jennifer closed her eyes and spun around three times, holding her hands straight down at her sides. As she spun round, she chanted:

> 'Xilka, Xilka, Besa, Besa;
> Xilka, Xilka, Besa, Besa;
> Xilka, Xilka, Besa, Besa.'

On the third spin, and with her eyes still closed, she pointed right at me. I walked into the magic circle, scared, shaking, and certainly not talking.

That was just the beginning of Elizabeth's fascinating friendship with Jennifer, the witch, the girl who could produce watermelons in January and toads in frozen March, and walk round corners and up and down curbs without ever looking down. As an apprentice witch she endured months of special diets, of charms and incantations, of investing all their bicycling time, cinema time, roller-skating time, and lounging-around-the-house time in their magical studies, until April came and it was time to try the flying spell ...

This is a deliciously macabre, deliciously comical story of the two earnest seekers after magical knowledge and is good for everyone over nine. It was runner-up for the Newbery Medal in 1968.

Cover design by Pat Marriott

Jennifer, Hecate, Macbeth, and me

Written and Illustrated by
E. L. Konigsburg

Puffin Books

Puffin Books, A Division of Penguin Books Ltd,
Harmondsworth, Middlesex, England
Penguin Books Australia Ltd, Ringwood.
Victoria, Australia

First published in the U.S.A., 1967
Published in Great Britain by
Macmillan & Co. Ltd, 1968
Published in Puffin Books 1973
Copyright © E. L. Konigsburg, 1967

Made and printed in Great Britain by
Richard Clay (The Chaucer Press) Ltd,
Bungay, Suffolk
Set in Linotype Pilgrim

To Paul, Laurie, and Ross for loving a witch

1

I first met Jennifer on my way to school. It was Halloween, and she was sitting in a tree. I was going back to school from lunch. This particular lunch hour was only a little different from usual because of Halloween. We were told to dress in costume for the school Halloween parade. I was dressed as a Pilgrim.

I always walked the back road to school, and I always walked alone. We had moved to the apartment house in town in September just before school started, and I walked alone because I didn't have anyone to walk with. I walked the back way because it passed through a little woods that I liked. Jennifer was sitting in one of the trees in this woods.

Our apartment house had grown on a farm about ten years before. There was still a small farm across the street; it included a big white house, a greenhouse, a caretaker's house, and a pump painted green without a handle. The greenhouse had clean windows; they shone in the sun. I could see only the roof windows from our second floor apartment. The rest were hidden by trees and shrubs. My mother never called the place a farm; she always called it THE ESTATE. It was old; the lady who owned it was old. She had given part of her land to the town for a park, and the town named the park after her: Samellson Park. THE ESTATE gave us a beautiful view from our apartment. My mother liked trees.

Our new town was not full of apartments. Almost everyone else lived in houses. There were only three apartment buildings as big as ours. All three sat on the top of the hill from the train station. Hundreds of men rode the train to New York City every morning and rode it home every night. My father did. In the mornings the elevators would be full of kids going to school and fathers going to the train. The kids left the building by the back door and ran down one side of the hill to the school. The fathers left the building by the front door and ran down the other side of the hill to the station.

Other kids from the apartment chose to walk to school through the little woods. The footsteps of all of them for ten years had worn away the soil so that the roots of the trees were bare and made steps for walking up and down the steep slope. The little woods made better company than the sidewalks. I liked the smells of the trees and the colours of the trees. I liked to walk with my head way up, practically hanging over my back. Then I could see the patterns the leaves formed against the blue sky.

I had my head way back and was watching the leaves when I first saw Jennifer up in the tree. She was dressed as a Pilgrim, too. I saw her feet first. She was sitting on one of the lower branches of the tree swinging her feet. That's how I happened to see her feet first. They were just about the boniest feet I had ever seen. Swinging right in front of my eyes as if I were sitting in the first row at Cinerama. They wore real Pilgrim shoes made of buckles and cracked old leather. The heel part flapped up and down because the shoes were so big that only the toe part could stay attached. Those shoes looked as if they were going to fall off any minute.

I grabbed the heel of the shoe and shoved it back on to the heel of that bony foot. Then I wiped my hands on my Pilgrim apron and looked up at Jennifer. I didn't

know yet that she was Jennifer. She was not smiling, and I was embarrassed.

I said in a loud voice, which I hoped would sound stout red but which came out sounding thin blue, 'You're going to lose that shoe.'

The first thing Jennifer ever said to me was, 'Witches never lose anything.'

'But you're not a witch,' I said. 'You're a Pilgrim, and look, so am I.'

'I won't argue with you,' she said. 'Witches convince; they never argue. But I'll tell you this much. Real witches are Pilgrims, and just because I don't have on a silly black costume and carry a silly broom and wear a silly black hat, doesn't mean that I'm not a witch. I'm a witch all the time and not just on Halloween.'

I didn't know what to say, so I said what my mother always says when she can't answer one of my questions. I said, 'You better hurry up now, or you'll be late for school.'

'Witches are never late,' she said.

'But witches have to go to school.' I wished I had said something clever.

'I just go to school because I'm putting the teacher under a spell,' she said.

'Which teacher?' I asked. 'Get it? *Witch* teacher?' I laughed. I was pleased that now I had said something clever.

Jennifer neither laughed nor answered. But I was sure she'd got it. She looked at me hard and said, 'Give me those three chocolate chip cookies, and I'll come down and tell you my name, and I'll walk the rest of the way to school with you.'

I wasn't particularly hungry for the cookies, but I was hungry for company, so I said, 'Okay,' and reached out my hand holding the cookies. I wondered how she could tell that they were chocolate chips. They were in a bag.

As she began to swing down from the branches, I caught a glimpse of her underwear. I expected that it would look dusty, and it did. But that was not why it was not like any underwear I had ever seen. It was old fashioned. There were buttons and no elastic. She also had on yards and yards of petticoats. Her Pilgrim dress looked older than mine. Much older. Much, much older. Hers looked ancient. Of course, my Pilgrim costume was not new either. I had worn it the year before, but then I had been in a different grade in a different school. My cousin had worn the costume before that. I hadn't grown much during the year. My dress was only a little short, and only a little tight, and only a little scratchy where it was pinned, and it was only absolutely uncomfortable. In other words, my costume was a hand-me-down, but Jennifer's was a genuine antique.

After Jennifer touched the ground, I saw that she was taller than I. Everybody was. I was the shortest kid in my class. I was always the shortest kid in my class. She was thin. Skinny is what she really was. She came towards my hand and looked hard at the bag of cookies.

'Are you sure you didn't bite any of them?' she demanded.

'Sure I'm sure,' I said. I was getting mad, but a bargain's a bargain.

'Well,' she said, taking one cookie out of the bag, 'My name is Jennifer. Now let's get going.' As she said 'going', she grabbed the bag with the other two cookies and started to walk.

'Wait up,' I yelled. 'A bargain's a bargain. Don't you want to know my name?'

'I told you witches are never late, but I can't be responsible for you yet . . . Elizabeth.'

She knew my name already! She walked so fast that I was almost convinced that she was a witch; she was practically flying. We got to school just as the tardy bell began to ring. Jennifer's room was a fifth grade just off the corridor near the entrance, and she slipped into her classroom while the bell was still buzzing. My room was four doors further down the hall, and I got to my room *after* the bell had stopped.

She had said that witches are never late. Being late felt as uncomfortable as my tight Pilgrim dress. No Pilgrim had ever suffered as much as I did. Walking to my seat while everyone stared at me was awful. My desk was in the back of the room; it was a long, long walk. The whole class had time to see that I was a blushing Pilgrim. I knew that I was ready to cry. The whole class didn't have to know that too, so I didn't raise my eyes until I was seated and felt sure that they wouldn't leak. When I looked up, I saw that there were six Pilgrims: three other Pilgrim girls and two Pilgrim boys. That's a lot of Pilgrims for a class of twenty. But none of them could be witches, I thought. After checking over their costumes and shoes, I decided that at least three of them had cousins who had been Pilgrims the year before.

Miss Hazen announced that she would postpone my

detention until the next day because of the Halloween parade. Detention was a school rule; if you were late coming to school, you stayed after school that day. The kids called it 'staying after'. I didn't feel grateful for the postponement. She could have skipped my 'staying after' altogether.

Our lesson that afternoon was short, and I didn't perform too well. I had to tug on my dress a lot and scratch

under my Pilgrim hat a lot. I would have scratched other places where the costume itched, but they weren't polite.

At last we were all lined up in the hall. Each class was to march to the auditorium and be seated. Then one class at a time would walk across the stage before the judges. The rest of the classes would be the audience. The classes at the end of the hall marched to the auditorium first.

There were classes on both sides of the hall near my room, and the space for the marchers was narrow. Some of the children had large cardboard cartons over them and were supposed to be packages of cigarettes or sports cars. These costumes had trouble getting through. Then there was Jennifer. She was last in line. She looked neither to the right nor to the left but slightly up towards the ceiling. I kept my eye on her hoping she'd say 'Hi' so that I wouldn't feel so alone standing there. She didn't. Instead, well, I almost didn't believe what I actually saw her do.

But before I tell what I saw her do, I have to tell about Cynthia. Every grown-up in the whole U.S. of A. thinks that Cynthia is perfect. She is pretty and neat and smart. I guess that makes perfect to almost any grown-up. Since she lives in the same apartment house as we do, and since my mother is a grown-up, and since my mother thinks that she is perfect, my mother had tried hard to have us become friends since we first moved to town. My mother would drop hints. HINT: Why don't you call Cynthia and ask her if she would like to show you where the library is? Then you can both eat lunch here. Or HINT: Why don't you run over and play with Cynthia while I unpack the groceries?

It didn't take me long to discover that what Cynthia was, was not perfect. The word for what Cynthia was, was *mean*.

Here's an example of mean. There was a little boy in our building who had moved in about a month before we did. His name was Johann; that's German for John. He moved from Germany and didn't speak English yet. He loved Cynthia. Because she was so pretty, I guess. He followed her around and said, 'Cynsssia, Cynsssia.' Cynthia always made fun of him. She would stick her tongue between her teeth and say, 'Th, th, th, th, th. My name is Cyn-*th*-ia not Cyn-*sss*-ia.' Johann would smile and say, 'Cyn-*sss*-ia.' Cynthia would stick out her tongue and say, 'Th, th, th, th, th.' And then she'd walk away from him. I liked Johann. I wished he would follow me around. I would have taught him English, and I would never even have minded if he called me Elizabessss. Another word for what Cynthia was, was *two-faced*. Because every time some grown-up was around, she was sweet to Johann. She'd smile at him and pat his head ... only until the grown-up left.

And another thing: Cynthia certainly didn't need me for a friend. She had a very good friend called Dolores who also lived in the apartment house. They told secrets and giggled together whenever I got into the elevator with them. So I got into the habit of leaving for school before they did. Sometimes, on weekends, they'd be in the elevator when I got on; I'd act as if they weren't there. I had to get off the elevator before they did because I lived on the second floor, and they lived on the sixth. Before I'd get off the elevator, I'd take my fists, and fast and furious, I'd push every floor button just the second before I got out. I'd step out of the elevator and watch the dial stopping at every floor on the way up. Then I'd skip home to our apartment.

For Halloween Cynthia wore everything real ballerinas wear : leotards and tights and ballet slippers and a tutu. A tutu is a little short skirt that ballerinas wear somewhere around their waists. Hers looked like a nylon net doughnut floating around her middle. Besides all the equipment I listed above, Cynthia wore rouge and eye make-up and lipstick and a tiara. She looked glamorous, but I could tell that she felt plenty chilly in that costume. Her teeth were chattering. She wouldn't put on a sweater.

As we were standing in the hall waiting for our turn to go to the auditorium, and as Jennifer's class passed, Cynthia was turned around talking to Dolores. Dolores was dressed as a Pilgrim. They were both whispering and giggling. Probably about Jennifer.

Here's what Jennifer did. As she passed Cynthia, she reached out and quicker than a blink unsnapped the tutu. I happened to be watching her closely, but even I didn't believe that she had really done it. Jennifer clop-clopped along in the line with her eyes still up towards the ceiling and passed me a note almost without my knowing. She did it so fast that I wasn't even sure she did it until I felt the note in my hand and crunched it beneath my apron to hide it. Jennifer never took her eyes off the ceiling or broke out of line for even half a step.

I wanted to make sure that everyone saw Cynthia with her tutu down, so I pointed my finger at her and said, 'O-o-o-o-oh!' I said it loud. Of course, that made everyone on both sides of the aisle notice her and start to giggle.

Cynthia didn't have sense enough to be embarrassed. She loved attention so much that she didn't care if her tutu had fallen. She stepped out of it, picked it up, shook it out, floated it over her head, and anchored it back around her waist. She touched her hands to her hair, giving it little pushes the way women do who have just come out of the beauty parlour. I hoped she was itchy.

Finally, our class got to the auditorium. After I sat

down, I opened the note, holding both my hands under my Pilgrim apron. I slowly slipped my hands out and glanced at the note. I was amazed at what I saw. Jennifer's note looked like this :

Meet for Trick or Treat at
Half after six P.M. o'clock of this evening.
By the same tree.
Bring two (2) bags.
Those were good cookies

I studied the note a long time. I thought about the note as I watched the Halloween parade; I wondered if Jennifer used a quill pen. You can guess that I didn't win any prizes for my costume. Neither did Cynthia. Neither did Jennifer (even though I thought she would have). We all marched across the stage wearing our masks and stopped for a curtsy or bow (depending on whether you were a girl or a boy) in front of the judges who were sitting at a table in the middle of the stage. Some of the girls who were disguised as boys forgot themselves and curtsied. Then we marched off. Our class was still seated when Jennifer clop-clopped across the stage in those crazy Pilgrim slippers. She didn't wear a mask at all. She wore a big brown paper bag over her head and *there were no holes cut out for her eyes*. Yet, she walked up the stairs, across the stage, stopped and curtsied, and walked off without tripping or falling or walking out of those gigantic shoes.

2 Our family rushed through supper that night. But the trick or treaters started coming even before we finished. Most of the early ones were bitsy kids who had to bring their mothers to reach the door bells for them.

I didn't tell my parents about Jennifer. I mentioned to my mother that I was meeting a friend at 6.30, and we were going to trick or treat together. Mom just asked, 'Someone from school?' and I just said, 'Yes.'

The days start getting short, and the evenings start getting cool in late October. So I had to wear my old ski jacket over my costume. I looked like a Pilgrim who had made a bad trade with the Indians. Jennifer was waiting. She was leaning against the tree. She had put on stockings. They were long, black, cotton stockings, and she wore a huge black shawl. She smelled a little bit like moth balls, but I happen to especially like that smell in autumn.

'Hi,' I said.

'I'll take the bigger bag,' she replied.

She didn't say 'please'.

I held out the bags. She took the bigger one. She didn't say 'thank you'. Her manners were unusual. I guessed that witches never said 'please' and never said 'thank you'. All my life my mother had taught me a politeness vocabulary. I didn't mind. I thought that 'please' and 'thank you' made conversation prettier, just as bows and lace make dresses prettier. I was full of admiration for how easily Jennifer managed without bows or lace or 'please' or 'thank you'.

She opened her bag, stuck her head way down inside, and said:

> 'Bag, sack, parcel post,
> Fill thyself
> With goodies most.'

She lifted her head out of the bag and tightened her shawl. 'We can go now,' she said.

'Don't you mean "Bag, sack, parcel, *poke?*" ' I asked. 'Parcel *post* is the mail; *poke* is a name for a bag.'

Jennifer was walking with her head up, eyes up. She shrugged her shoulders and said, 'Poetic licence. *Poke* doesn't rhyme.'

I shrugged my shoulders and started walking with her. Jennifer disappeared behind a tree. No master spirit had taken her away. She reappeared in a minute, pulling a wagon. It was the usual kind of child's wagon, but to make the sides taller, she had stretched a piece of chicken wire all along the inner rim. Jennifer pulled the wagon, carried her bag, clutched her shawl, and clop-clopped towards the first house. I walked.

I had been trick or treating for a number of years. I began as a bitsy kid, and my mother rang the door bells for me, as other mothers were ringing them for those other bitsy kids that night. I had been a nurse, a mouse (I had worn my sleepers with the feet in), and other things. I had been a Pilgrim before, too. I mentioned that I had been a Pilgrim the year before. All I mean to say is that I'd been trick or treating for years and years and years, and I'd seen lots of trick or treaters come to our house, but I'd never, never, never seen a performance like Jennifer's.

This is the way Jennifer operated: 1. She left the wagon outside the door of the house and out of sight of

her victim. 2. She rang the bell. 3. Instead of smiling and
saying 'trick or treat', she said nothing when the people
came to the door. 4. She half fell against the door post
and said, 'I would like just a drink of water.' 5. She
breathed hard. 6. The lady or man who answered would
say, 'Of course,' and would bring her a drink of water. 7.
As she reached out to get the water, she dropped her big,

empty bag. 8. The lady or man noticed how empty it was and said, 'Don't you want just a little something?' 9. The lady or man poured stuff into Jennifer's bag. 10. The lady or man put a little something in my bag, too. 11. Jennifer and I left the house. 12. Jennifer dumped the treats into the wagon. 13. Jennifer clop-clopped to the next house with the bag empty again. 14. I walked.

Jennifer did this at every house. She always drank a glass of water. She always managed to drop her empty bag. I asked her how she could drink so much water. She must have had about twenty-four glasses. She didn't answer. She shrugged her shoulders and walked with her head up, eyes up. I sort of remembered something about a water test for witches. But I also sort of remembered that it was something about witches being able to float on water that was outside their bodies, not water that was inside their bodies.

I asked Jennifer why she didn't wear a mask. She answered that one disguise was enough. She told me that all year long she was a witch, disguised as a perfectly normal girl; on Halloween she became undisguised. She may be a witch, I thought, and, of course, she was a girl. But perfect never! And normal never!

I can say that Jennifer collected more treats on that Halloween than I had in all my years put together including the time I was a mouse in my sleepers with the feet in. Because I was with Jennifer each time she went into her act, I managed to collect more treats on that Halloween than I ever had before but not nearly as many as Jennifer. My bag was heavy, though.

Jennifer and I parted about a block from my apartment house. My bag was so heavy that I could hardly hold it with one hand as I pushed the button for the elevator. I put the bag on the floor while I waited. When the elevator arrived, I leaned over to pick up my bundle and heard my Pilgrim dress go *r-r-r-r-r-r-i-p*. I arrived at our apartment, tired and torn, but happy. Happy because I had had a successful Halloween; happy because I had not met Cynthia on the elevator; and happy because my costume had ripped. I wouldn't have to be an itchy Pilgrim another Halloween.

3

School went very well the next day. We played
dodge ball in gym; I got Cynthia out. I aimed a good one
right at the back of her legs; it almost knocked her over.
It wasn't much fun getting after Cynthia in front of the
teacher, though. Since the teacher was a grown-up, Cynthia acted sweet. She smiled when she got called out and
pretended that it was the nicest thing that had ever happened to her.

I didn't mind 'staying after' that day. It was cloudy
and chilly. There was nothing special to do during the
afternoon, and no one special to do it with. Miss Hazen
made me write 'I will not be tardy' one hundred times. I
used a lot of time doing it. I practised all different kinds
of printing and all different kinds of writing. A couple of
times I tried to write as Jennifer did but decided that I
would need something more special than a ball point
pen. I numbered the lines in Roman numerals, and that
took a lot of time. I had to figure out whether 49 should
be XXXXIX or XLIX or IL. I'm sure I enjoyed my punish-
ment much more than Miss Hazen did. Maybe she
wished she had made me write it only fifty times. She
would say things like, 'You'll just have to go faster,' or
'Are you almost ready?' or 'You work much faster than
this usually.'

I finished. Walking home alone seemed less lonely
when there weren't a lot of other kids walking in two's
and three's. Even the cop who guards the school crossing

had gone off duty. I was walking calmly and patiently; that's the way I was feeling. Miss Hazen zoomed past me in her car. She didn't notice when I waved to her. When you're driving that fast, I guess you have to concentrate on steering. I'll bet she was glad that the cop was gone. The little woods said November now; maybe because it was cloudy.

A little way into the woods I spotted a note tacked to the Jennifer tree. For me! For me! I knew it was for me. It was written on brownish paper in Jennifer's peculiar handwriting. It said:

Library Reading Room
Saturday 10:00 A. M. o'clock
of the morning

I folded the note and left the tack in the tree. Then I zoomed the rest of the way home wishing that it could be Saturday in five minutes.

The rest of that week seemed to have a month's worth of days, but Saturday came. It was a golden day full of the smells of autumn. I told my parents that I'd skip going grocery shopping with them. I told them that I had some work to do at the library. No argument. I was usually a nag for them to take to the supermarket. I wasn't very popular at the supermarket either. Once I had rammed the cart into a big mountain of cracker boxes. Avalanche! I told the manager that I'd pick them all up, and I did. I arranged them very artistically; the aisle was blocked for forty-five minutes. I hadn't been very popular at that supermarket since.

When I got to the library reading room, I knew Jennifer was already there. Her wagon was parked by the encyclopedias. She was looking at a big book of maps when I came in. Libraries are for whispering, and I soon discovered that Jennifer whispered beautifully, with many nice sssssssssssss sounds coming out like steam out of a kettle.

I whispered, 'Hi.'

She whispered back, 'Did you bring something to eat?'

'No,' I said. 'Supermarket day. The cupboard was bare.'

She closed the atlas and looked at me for what seemed like a very long time. Leaning way over and in such a quiet voice that it was almost zero, she said, 'I've decided to make you an apprentice witch.'

'What do I have to do?' I asked.

'Answer "yes" or "no".' I must have looked worried. She didn't let me waste time; she came across soft but fast. 'If you really want to be a witch, nothing you have to do will seem like too much. If you don't really want to be a witch, everything will seem like too much. Answer "yes" or "no".'

I answered, 'Yes.'

'We'll start today,' she said and got down from her chair. She replaced the huge book of maps on its proper shelf before pulling the wagon towards the check-out table. The wagon was loaded with seven heavy, large books. She handed these up to the librarian one at a time and then replaced each one in the wagon after it had been checked out.

The librarian said to Jennifer, 'Did you finish last week's supply?' I guessed that Jennifer was well known at the library.

Jennifer sighed and said, 'Of course.' She grabbed the handle of the wagon and pulled it out the door and down the steps to the street. Those steps are steep. But not a single book fell out of Jennifer's wagon on the bumpity way down.

That Saturday Jennifer was dressed as she was usually dressed for school. That is, she wore a skirt. I later learned that she never wore jeans or shorts. She always wore a skirt. It was always an ordinary skirt. There was one thing about the way she was dressed that Saturday that was unordinary. Around her neck she had a gigantic key. She had it hanging from an old yo-yo string. The wagon was heavy with her books. Jennifer had to pull it with both hands behind her, and she had to lean way over to make the wagon move. That made the key hang very low; it would clung the sidewalk every now and then.

We headed for Samellson Park. We didn't talk much on the way. I didn't ask Jennifer where she lived and whether she had any brothers and sisters and where her father worked. She didn't ask me either. I suspected she knew everything about me anyway. There wasn't too much to know. I am an only child.

When we got to the park, we walked towards the fountain. First, Jennifer took a drink. I'd never seen anyone love water the way Jennifer did. Then we sat down on one of the benches nearby. The water fountain was in the centre of a cement circle. There were paths leading to it from four different sides of the park. I'd guess that the circle was about nine feet across. I soon learned that much as she loved water, Jennifer was more interested in the cement circle than she was in the fountain.

'Now, if you're ready,' she said, 'we'll begin.'

I would have been more ready if Jennifer had not seemed so serious. She was as serious as a doctor ready to give me a DPT booster shot. A witch doctor, I thought. When I answered, I tried to sound firm and a little bit annoyed, the way Jennifer did with the librarian. I said, 'Of course.' Jennifer could not be imitated. My voice came out loud Elizabeth instead of cool Jennifer.

Jennifer took a piece of chalk out of her pocket and

made a chalk mark all around the edge of the concrete circle. That crazy key kept scraping along the concrete as she bent over. I hoped that after I became a witch's apprentice, I wouldn't get goose pimples from that noise any more. After the whole circle was completed, Jennifer took a candle from her pocket. She lit it and stuck the candle on to the concrete near the bottom of the fountain by dripping some of the wax first. After standing there with her eyes wide open, staring at the big sky, she marched out of the circle straight over to me.

'Watch me,' she said. 'When I'm ready, I'll point to

you. When I point to you, you may enter the magic circle. But be quiet. Don't sneeze, burp, or breathe loud. Also, don't talk.'

Then Jennifer walked back to as near centre as she could get without actually standing inside the fountain. She closed her eyes and spun around three times, holding her hands straight down at her sides. As she spun around, she chanted:

> 'Xilka, Xilka, Besa, Besa;
> Xilka, Xilka, Besa, Besa;
> Xilka, Xilka, Besa, Besa.'

On the third spin, and with her eyes still closed, she pointed right at me. I walked into the magic circle, scared, shaking, and certainly not talking.

Jennifer took the big key from around her neck, twirled it over her head, and laid it on the ground near the centre of the circle. Next she took a pin out of her pocket. She pricked her finger; and without even asking permission, she pricked mine, too. Holding her hand over mine, she placed both our hands on the key. Each of our fingers dripped a drop of blood on to it. Jennifer picked it up, spit on it, and handed it to me. So I spit on it, too. She held the key over the candle to dry the spit and the blood. The candle made crackle sounds as she did this. When the key was dry she put it back down on the concrete and blew out the candle. Then she took her forefinger that had been pricked and hooked it to my forefinger that had been pricked. We marched around the key three times before she stopped and picked it up. Holding it out by the yo-yo string, she chanted:

'So thee and me shall never part,
Wear this key around thy heart.'

Jennifer put the key around my neck. The yo-yo string was so long that the key hung not around 'thy heart' but around 'thy knees'. Looking me hard in the eyes she stuck out her pricked forefinger. I stuck out mine. We hooked our fingers together and shook them up and down three times and did another marching around the magic circle.

I was so impressed with the ceremony that I still didn't want to say anything to break the magic spell. The big key kept clunging me on the knees. I waited until we walked out of the magic circle and were standing back at the bench before I said, 'Don't you think this string is a little long? Unless now that I'm an apprentice my heart has slipped down to my knees.' I laughed at my little joke. Jennifer didn't laugh.

She said, 'I got it from a very tall witch.'

'May I shorten it some?' I asked.

She replied, 'You can tie it up, but don't cut it.'

I lost no time tying it up so that it hung over my heart. My knees already felt black and blue.

Then Jennifer said, 'For the first week of your apprenticeship you must eat a raw egg every day. And you must bring me an egg every day. Make mine hard boiled. And you must read this book about witchcraft; it tells about some of my famous relatives. They were hanged in Salem, Massachusetts.'

I said, 'A *raw* egg?'

She said, 'I knew you'd ask that. R-A-W. Leave my egg by the tree. See you next week.'

And that's the way Jennifer and I parted that first Saturday. We walked in opposite directions. I looked back after I had taken only a few steps. I couldn't see either Jennifer or her wagon. They had disappeared.

All the way home I thought about my friend, Jennifer, the witch. I also thought that I had gone out an ordinary girl and had come back a witch's apprentice. I didn't feel different except that I felt like throwing up every time I thought of eating a raw egg. Every day! *For a week!*

4

How I managed to eat a raw egg every day the next week was less of a mystery than what happened to the hard boiled eggs I left for Jennifer. I left the egg every morning on my way to school. On two mornings I left our apartment so late that I was almost tardy for school again. But when I walked home at noon, the egg was always gone. There was always a little brown piece of paper with the words:

Received one (1) egg

I wondered how she managed to pick up the egg and still get to school on time. I never saw her that week.

Here's how I solved the problem of the raw egg: milkshakes, that's how. My mother didn't usually make milkshakes because I am what is known as a fussy eater. Such as I won't eat anything cooked with tomato sauce. I won't eat the crusts of bread, and I won't even taste anything with mayonnaise. I never eat eggs. Even when I was a little baby before I knew better, I knew better. I never ate eggs then either. Poached or boiled, scrambled or broiled, I never eat eggs.

Every day that week I asked for a milkshake. My mother would say 'no.' Then I'd say that I'd like her to break an egg into it. She'd be delighted at that. I'd drink my milkshake and hardly know I was drinking a raw egg.

I'd boil the egg for Jennifer the night before and keep it in my underwear drawer until morning. I read parts of *The Black Book of Witchcraft*, but I couldn't finish it. It was an encyclopedia. I read about the Pilgrim witches in Salem, Massachusetts. One of them was Captain John Alden, who was the son of Priscilla and speak-for-yourself John. Some of them were little kids. Just like Jennifer; just like me. Some of them were hanged.

The weather was getting colder, and I was ordered to add layer after layer of clothes. I didn't mind. If my mother said to put on ear muffs, I put on ear muffs. If my mother said to put on knee socks, I put on knee socks. Each trip to and from school had become an adventure. Dressing for that adventure became exciting, too. My mother was amazed; she said that I was acting like a different child. Of course, I was a different child. She thought the eggs were responsible.

On Friday I found two notes. One was about the egg, and one was about meeting in the reading room of the library again. So it happened that we got to meeting in the library every Saturday morning 'at 10.00 A.M. o'clock of the morning', as Jennifer said. We'd check out our books. I usually took out one book besides renewing *The Black Book of Witchcraft*. Jennifer always took out seven books. I could tell that the librarian liked Jennifer even though Jennifer never said 'hello' or 'good-bye' or 'please' or 'thank you'. Librarians love good readers, and Jennifer was that. In fact, Jennifer wasn't just a good reader, Jennifer was a *serious* reader.

After we'd checked out our books, we would dump them into Jennifer's wagon. Both of us would pull the wagon to the magic circle in the park. She always parked the wagon near the bench outside the magic circle. Then Jennifer and I would hook our forefingers

together and silently march around three times; the first time slowly, the second time mediumly, and the third time rapidly. We talked about witches in colonial days and the man who liked to hang witches in colonial days: Cotton Mather. We talked about plants that eat insects: insectivorous. We talked about the painter who cut off his ear: Van Gogh. We talked about the guillotine in France, about being shipwrecked on an island without water, about lice and the bubonic plague, and other interesting things.

Every week I ate a different special food and left some kind of food by the Jennifer tree. I didn't always leave the same food for Jennifer. Apprentice witches have much stricter diets than master witches. One week I had to drink black coffee every day; Jennifer said hers would spill, so we settled on coffee cake for Jennifer. Other foods I had to eat every day were:

> ¼ cup uncooked oatmeal; Jennifer got
>   ¼ cup sugar frosted flakes.
> 1 raw hot dog; Jennifer got the same.

My mother was not always too patient about my food habits. She couldn't understand why I wanted a hot dog for lunch every day, especially an uncooked one. But I had this reputation for being a fussy eater. Besides, I was an only child; besides, I was a nag.

Soon it was Thanksgiving weekend. It was on Thanksgiving Saturday that Jennifer decided we should make a magic ointment. There were three main kinds of ointments:

> Ointments that make you fly
> Ointments that change you into an animal
> Ointments that kill people

'Let's not kill anyone,' I said.

'Okay,' Jennifer answered.

'Let's make the ointment that will change us into another animal,' I said. 'I'd enjoy changing into a giraffe. I'd be tall, and I'd have beautiful brown eyes.'

'They can't make any noise. They don't have a larynx, which is a voice box,' Jennifer said. 'If I'm going to be an animal, I'm going to be a noisy one. Or else a fast one. I'll be a panther; they're fast.'

'But all the panthers and all the giraffes in the whole U.S. of A. live in zoos. We'd be caged! Do you suppose we should become loose animals?'

Jennifer thought a minute and said, 'I'll be a cougar.'

'What's that?' I asked.

'A western wildcat,' she answered.

I thought a minute and said, 'I'll take a French poodle; they're smart dogs, and I've always wanted curly hair.'

Jennifer gave me a sharp look and said, 'If I'm a wild-cat and you're a poodle, we're going to fight like cat and dog.'

'Okay,' I said, 'you change.'

She answered, 'I said cougar before you said French poodle.'

'But I said change first.' Jennifer said nothing. I waited, then I said, 'Besides, being first doesn't make you right.' Jennifer said nothing; so I continued, 'People first believed that the world was flat; being first didn't make them right. It doesn't make you right either.' Jennifer still said nothing. I waited.

She looked straight ahead. At last she spoke. She said, 'Cougar.'

I said, 'Poodle.'

She said, 'Cougar.'

I said, 'Poodle.'

Then she said nothing. And I said nothing. She wouldn't argue. She began to read the *Black Book*. We were just *thinking* about changing into cougar and poodle, and we were fighting. Imagine how unfriendly we'd be when we actually changed! I was ready to admit that I should become a Siamese cat. Before I said so, Jennifer looked up from the *Black Book* and said, 'There's no way we can pick which animal we'll be. Suppose we both become mosquitoes.'

'I know who I'll bite first,' I said looking straight at her.

Jennifer didn't notice. She was still looking at the *Black Book*. 'We could both easily lose our lives to DDT or even a fly-swatter. Let's make the flying ointment.'

'Fine with me,' I said. We turned the pages of the book to find out how to make the ointment. The witches didn't ever give the exact ingredients. So Jennifer gave me a new assignment. I was to read the *Black Book* very carefully and make a list of all the possible ingredients that could go into a flying ointment. She said that she would find out what chants to chant when we spread the ointment on ourselves.

'Where are you going to find out?' I asked. Jennifer didn't answer. She shrugged her shoulders and looked up. I got mad. Some days I got really mad at Jennifer. Some days I really didn't like being her apprentice. But I was always a little bit worried that she would choose another apprentice. Sometimes when I got angry like this, I'd say to myself, 'Who does she think she is, anyway?' And I'd answer, 'She's Jennifer.'

Before I'd got Jennifer, I'd had no one. In the days before Jennifer, I would talk to Tony, the janitor in our building. He was a very usual kind of person; he'd always say something about the weather first. 'Cold today.' 'Cheely again.' 'Wew! itsa hota one.' Then he'd say something about his work. 'Them boys oughta getta boot for dirting up thisa place.' After talking to Tony only a couple of times I knew everything. Such as how many kids he had and which ones were 'gooda boys'. I knew even before September was over. He liked questions and answered all of them as long as I stayed polite. Imagine Jennifer doing that!

I could ask her questions until I was indigo in the face. (Indigo is deeper than blue.) She still wouldn't tell me. I knew she wouldn't tell me, so actually I never tried very hard.

After all, she had chosen me because she knew that I had all the makings of a fine witch. That must have been why she chose me. And I knew that she was a fine witch already. When you understand something that important about someone, you don't have to know a lot of other stuff. Like does she have to dry the dishes after supper, and what kind of house does she live in. Besides, even if I did find out all this usual, Tony kind of stuff and discovered that Jennifer lived in an ordinary house and did ordinary things, I would know that it was a disguise.

So I got mad, but I didn't stay mad. Every time I thought I couldn't eat one more apprentice food, I would eat it. I wanted to be a witch so bad that I would eat it. There was a lot I didn't find out about her and a lot I gave in to. But it was worth it. Being an apprentice witch was worth it. Besides, I thought how nice it would be to fly.

The next week, Jennifer said I was to eat a raw onion every day. I was to leave her a raw carrot, peeled, wrapped in Saran, and slightly salted.

5

The minute we got back from Thanksgiving weekend, the whole school started getting ready for Christmas and the Christmas play. Especially our grade. This year the fifth grade was to put on the play. The play is always presented twice; once for the whole school and once for the Parent and Teachers Association meeting at night. There are three fifth grade classes in William McKinley Elementary School; that's my school. Three fifth grades adds up to about sixty kids. All the other classes of William McKinley Elementary School were to sing carols and recite poems.

That first Monday afternoon after Thanksgiving all the fifth graders met in the auditorium. Each classroom teacher had read the play in the morning. Mrs Stuyvestant would direct the play; Mrs Stuyvestant would choose the cast for the play; Mrs Stuyvestant had written the play. The play was long. It had to be long so that all sixty kids could get a chance to act. Our school was democratic about Christmas. Here's the play:

There is a king who lives once upon a time (of course). He has a beautiful daughter (of course). He loves his beautiful daughter very much (of course). She is very unhappy. No one knows why she is very unhappy. The king wants to make her happy, so he asks her what can he give her for Christmas. She doesn't know (of course). The king goes to Santa's workshop, and he asks Santa what can he give his beautiful, unhappy daughter for Christmas. Santa's workshop is full of merry elves who all love the princess like crazy. They are all hammering and sawing and carrying on. Santa holds up all these dolls and things, but the king doesn't think they will make the princess smile. He shakes his head and walks away. Then the king goes to the queen's chamber, and he asks the queen what can he give their beautiful, unhappy daughter for Christmas. The queen's chamber is full of beautiful ladies-in-waiting who all love the princess like crazy. They are all singing and dancing and carrying on. The queen holds up all these clothes and things, but the king doesn't think they will make the princess smile. He shakes his head and walks away. Then the king goes to the kitchen, and he asks the chef what can he give his beautiful, unhappy daughter for Christmas. The kitchen is full of cook's helpers who all love the princess like crazy. They are all stirring big pots and being jolly and carrying on. The chef holds up all these cakes and cookies and things, but the king doesn't think they will make the princess smile. He shakes his head and walks away. He walks to his throne room. He sits down to think. He thinks and thinks. He thinks he has a real problem. Soon an old scrub woman comes in. She looks so happy scrubbing that the king thinks she has an answer to unhappiness. He asks her what can he give his beautiful, unhappy daughter for Christmas. She tells him that he should give the beautiful, unhappy princess a puppy because to be happy you have to love and take care of someone as well as be loved and be taken care of. She tells him that that is one of the lessons of Christmas. The king thinks this is a great idea. He gets his beautiful, unhappy princess a puppy (of course). She smiles happily (of course), and the play is over (at last).

Guess who was the beautiful princess? Cynthia (of

course). Guess who was the little puppy? The smallest kid in the class. Me (of course). Jennifer was a lady-in-waiting. I couldn't tell whether she enjoyed being a lady or not. She kept her eyes up the whole time Mrs Stuyvestant was choosing the cast. No one knew that Jennifer and I had made a pact sealed in blood. No one knew that we were witch and apprentice or that we even knew each other. Witchcraft is a private affair. Very private. It's secret.

Remember that my apprentice food that week was one raw onion per day. It was no problem because I love onion sandwiches. I loved onion sandwiches even before I was a witch's apprentice ... when I was an ordinary, fussy eater. Here is my recipe for onion sandwiches: toast the bread, butter it, slice the onions, salt them, place them on the buttered slice of toast and cover with an unbuttered slice, cut off the crusts (of course) and eat. Delicious. On Sunday I had announced to my mother that I would be having an onion sandwich for lunch every day the next week.

'*Every* day?' my mother asked.

'Yes, *every* day,' I answered.

'Hot dogs last week; onions this week. There must be some special reason,' she said.

'There is,' I answered. My voice was trailing because I was stalling for time to think of a reason.

'Tell me,' my mother said. I could tell her patience was small because her voice was very slow and very patient. My father was home. That was the way she talked when she was angry if my father was home.

I thought fast. 'I am conducting an experiment. I think I can keep from catching a cold for a whole year if I eat one onion a day for a whole week before winter officially begins.'

'Well,' my mother said, 'you'll surely keep from catching cold for the week if not for the whole year. No one will be able to get close enough to give you any germs.' Her voice was still slow and low.

'Please, may I try it?' I asked.

'Thank goodness you don't know about asafoetida,' she said.

'What's asafoetida?' I asked.

'I'll never tell,' she answered.

I believe that if you like onions, you should love onions. Nice people love onions. If you love onions, you should find the odour of onions on someone's breath very pleasant.

Our first full rehearsal for the Christmas play was on Friday afternoon. It was a long rehearsal. All the teachers except Mrs Stuyvestant took coffee breaks. Everyone had to be prompted. Everyone stood in the wrong places. Mrs Stuyvestant would bounce up on stage and move the people around. She made chalk marks on the stage where they were to stand. By the end of that first rehearsal the floor looked like our classroom blackboard just after Miss Hazen explained long division by the New Math. Mrs Stuyvestant was the tallest woman I have ever seen. Everyone called her Mrs Sky-high-vestant.

My part was towards the end of the play. The king brings me (the puppy) to Cynthia (the princess). I didn't have any lines to memorize. My role meant putting on an old doggie costume and crawling around on all fours. And making bow-wow sounds. When the king gives me (the puppy) to Cynthia (the princess), Mrs Stuyvestant said that I was to stand up on my hind legs and put my hands (paws) on Cynthia's lap, look up at her face, stick out my tongue, and pant. 'Pant with excitement,' Mrs Stuyvestant said. 'Frolic around,' Mrs Stuyvestant said. I was afraid that Mrs Stuyvestant would ask me to wag my tail. Cynthia (the princess) was to snuggle her head up to mine and smile. Then everyone from Santa's workshop, from the Queen's chamber, and from the royal kitchen was to come back on stage and sing and dance and carry on.

Even though this was not a dress rehearsal for anyone else, I had to be in costume to get used to walking on all fours. Mrs Stuyvestant said that, too. The puppy costume was made of some fuzzy black orlon stuff that was thick, heavy, and hot. Inside, it smelled like a small glue factory. We rehearsed the elves and the ladies-in-waiting and the cooks. Long before I had to walk onstage, I was so hot inside the costume that I was sure I was going to commit spontaneous combustion. But I had heard that the show must go on. Mrs Stuyvestant said that. The only thing I did, the only thing I could do, was to unzip the head part of my costume and fling it back like a hood. I got some relief. Since this was only a rehearsal and no one else was in costume, I figured that it didn't make any difference.

Cynthia had been on stage almost the whole rehearsal. The king keeps visiting her during the play to see if she is smiling yet. She smiled the whole time she was on stage. She was supposed to be unhappy, but she was grinning. She wasn't laughing. Just grinning. Like the Mona Lisa. Mrs Stuyvestant would say, 'Be unhappy.' Cynthia would frown; but soon the grin would creep back over her face. She was grinning when the king brought me in.

The king announced, 'Princess, it is Christmas now, and it was Christmas then ... when you last smiled. Here is our gift. We give you this puppy with our love for you to love.' Then the king took me (the puppy) up to the princess. I put my hands (paws) on her lap. I stuck out my tongue. I panted. Cynthia, who had been grinning when she was not supposed to, was now supposed to smile very large. Large enough for the audience in the back rows to see, Mrs Stuyvestant said. Cynthia took a deep breath and began to snuggle her head up to mine. Instead of sighing and smiling, she stopped the sigh and

the smile and puffed out her cheeks like the old North Wind and clamped her hands over her nose and mouth and ran from the stage. Mrs Stuyvestant ran after her. I don't know what they discussed off stage, but Mrs Stuyvestant came back to me and sniffed me and asked me to kindly take the puppy costume home and have my mother kindly launder it, and she asked me to kindly not eat raw onions before rehearsals. Since this was Friday, the end of my onion week, I kindly agreed.

Jennifer was off stage. As I walked away, I saw a Mona Lisa smile on *her* face. She winked. No one saw that but me.

We had rehearsals every gym period, every music period, and every art period. They didn't call it 're-hearsal' during art period because we stayed in the art room and painted the sets and made cardboard crowns (covered with aluminium foil, glued and sprinkled with glitter dust). For the kitchen scene we made a stove out of big cardboard cartons that we painted black. It looked nice from the back rows where the audience sat. It looked nicest from the very last row. Mrs Stuyvestant asked each of us to bring in a cookie sheet or a pan or a kettle or a stirring spoon. We were to be sure to put our names on what we brought in so that we could get it back when the play was over. I brought in two cupcake pans and put one letter of my name on the inside of each cupcake hole. It looked like this:

I hoped that the whole audience, even the very last row would see. Mrs Stuyvestant asked me to kindly wash it off and kindly Scotch tape my name on the bottom—very small. She said, 'In the theatre one does not get top billing just because one can write one's name very large. One gets top billing because one has earned stardom.' One always knew when Mrs Stuyvestant was scolding because she always called you *one* instead of your name.

Cynthia brought in her mother's electric mixer. She knew that she was the only kid in the whole U.S. of A. whose mother would let her carry the family's electric mixer to school. Mrs Stuyvestant told her that it was very generous of her mother to lend it, and it was very generous of her to have carried it all the way from home. (I knew that Cynthia's mother had driven her to school that day, but Cynthia didn't mention it. Another example of the way Cynthia was: two-faced.) But Mrs Stuyvestant didn't consider the mixer picturesque enough. In other words, in the days when there were kings and princesses, there just weren't any electric mixers. Cynthia didn't even have sense enough to be insulted. She sighed sadly and told Mrs Stuyvestant that she would manage to get the mixer home, somehow, even though it was heavy.

Jennifer caused a small sensation. She brought in a huge black three-legged pot. It would hold about twenty quarts of water. A little kid could swim in it almost. Jennifer didn't have to write her name on that pot to identify it. No one else had ever seen anything like it except in a museum. I happened to know that it was the pot we were going to cook our flying ointment in.

Mrs Stuyvestant was overjoyed. She put her hands on her waist (with her elbows pointing out and her toes pointing out, too, she looked like a long, tall, five-pointed star) and exclaimed, 'Oh, Jenny, how *won*-derful! It's *too* cute! A *three*-legged kettle!'

If you ever want to make Jennifer angry, call her what Mrs Stuyvestant did. Call her Jenny instead of Jennifer, her rightful name.

Jennifer looked up, way up at Mrs Sky-high-vestant and said, 'That makes one, two, three, doesn't it?'

Mrs Stuyvestant looked down, way down at Jennifer and said, 'What do you mean, Jennifer?'

Jennifer answered, '*Won*-derful, *too* cute, *three*-legged. That's one, two, three.' Jennifer didn't smile.

Mrs Stuyvestant said, 'I had no idea you were so clever.' She smiled. I could tell that Jennifer wished that Mrs Stuyvestant had not smiled. She wanted her to notice how angry she was at being called Jenny instead of Jennifer.

Everyone was a little surprised at how clever Jennifer was. She almost never spoke in class or during rehearsals. She never spoke to me; she would just slip me a note every now and then. I was worried that everyone would find out how clever Jennifer was. It feels wonderful to have a secret. Sometimes I thought I wanted our secret to be discovered accidentally, but I didn't want to share Jennifer with the entire fifth grade. It was lucky, the kids of William McKinley Elementary School weren't ready to make the discovery. They were no longer paying any attention. Mrs Stuyvestant walked all around the pot, pleased and smiling. She smiled over at Jennifer and asked, 'By the way, Jenny, how did you get it here?' She was still feeling cozy towards Jennifer.

Jennifer pretended that she didn't hear the question. She was making herself very busy shaking a can of spray paint, and that little ball inside the can was rattling away. Mrs Stuyvestant said, 'Jenny. Oh, Jenny!' No answer from you-know-who. 'Jenny. Oh, Jenny!' No answer from you-know-who again. Mrs Stuyvestant started walking towards Jennifer and said, 'Jenny. Oh, Jennifer!' The minute she said *Jennifer*, you-know-who looked up.

'Yes?' asked Jennifer.

'I was wondering,' Mrs Stuyvestant said, 'how you got that heavy kettle to school.'

'Brought it in my wagon,' answered Jennifer.

'Then your wagon is parked at school?' asked Mrs Stuyvestant.

'Yes,' answered Jennifer.

'Do you think that you can lend it to Cynthia to help her get her mixer home?'

Jennifer asked, 'You want me to put the mixer in my wagon?'

Mrs Stuyvestant said, almost sarcastically, 'That's what I had in mind.'

Jennifer replied, 'I'll be happy to.'

Mrs Stuyvestant said, 'Thank you.' She smiled pleasantly at Jennifer and began to turn around.

Before she was completely turned around, Jennifer said, 'Do you think I should tie my wagon to the bumper?'

Mrs Stuyvestant spun around. 'The bumper? Bumper? The bumper of what?'

Jennifer answered, 'The bumper of their car.'

Mrs Stuyvestant was too puzzled to get angry. She merely asked. 'Why do that?'

Jennifer answered, 'Because Cynthia brought the mixer here in their car, so I guessed that that was the way she would get it home, too.' Somehow, Jennifer managed to look innocent.

Mrs Stuyvestant looked at Jennifer. Mrs Stuyvestant looked at Cynthia. Of course, Jennifer's conversation had been just one shade on the safe side of fresh. But Cynthia's conversation had been just one shade on the safe side of lying. Mrs Stuyvestant looked from Jennifer to

Cynthia and then back again. She threw her arms in the air, turned around, and walked out of the room. Cynthia glared at Jennifer. Jennifer kept shaking the spray paint and kept looking up at the ceiling.

'Oh, Jennifer,' I thought to myself, 'how strong you are. Nerves of steel and the heart of a witch!'

No one noticed when Jennifer passed me a note later in the period. I was painting hinges on one of the oven doors. The note had only one word on it. It said:

Ugh !!!

I knew what Jennifer meant, and I put my head inside the oven and laughed and laughed.

We got through the two performances of the play. They seemed short. Like standing over a stove all day long cooking up some very elegant soup, adding hundreds of special ingredients, stirring and stirring, and then having everyone gulp it down in five minutes.

The performance in front of the school wasn't as glamorous as the one for the Parent and Teachers Association at night. For one thing, the auditorium wouldn't get dark. For another thing, some of the kindergarten kids and the first graders who had sisters or brothers in the play would yell out, 'Hi, Johnny,' or 'Hello, Sis.' Only Richard yelled back. He was a cook in the kitchen scene; he stood on stage and shook a wooden spoon at his little brother in the audience and yelled, 'Mom told you not to call me.' Mrs Stuyvestant talked to all of us after this performance. She told us about how in the theatre one never lets the audience know how one feels. One always acts as if the world begins and ends at the edge of the stage. She talked on some more about *one* and *the theatre*, but Richard just sat there and bit his nails. He didn't know which *one* she meant.

The evening performance for the P. and T.A. went much better. Richard's little brother stayed home. I saw Jennifer's mother sitting in the audience. I knew it was Jennifer's mother because she was the only Negro mother there. She looked as normal as mine. Maybe she wasn't a witch.

Maybe witchery skipped generations as blue eyes do. All of a sudden blue eyes can pop up. That is like my brown-eyed uncle who married my brown-eyed aunt and who had a blue-eyed daughter named Emma. Maybe a normal mother and a normal father can give birth to a witch daughter named Jennifer. Of course, I didn't see her father since fathers almost never come to P. and T.A. meetings. Maybe Jennifer inherited being a witch from her father. Maybe Jennifer's father was a wizard, which is a boy witch.

6 This was my first Christmas vacation living in our apartment; it was pretty dull. No fireplace. No chimney. A lot of relatives came visiting and pinching. They always pinched my cheek and hugged me and kissed me and asked, 'Don't you have a kiss for your Aunt Buzzie? You remember how you used to always call me Aunt Buzzie because you couldn't pronounce Beatrice?' They thought that I was still small because I was still little. They didn't realize that although my size hadn't caught up with my age, my brain had. Still I always had a kiss for Aunt So and So who asked. And I always stayed still for the hugging, but I escaped a lot of cheek pinching that year. Just as they would lift their hands to pinch me, I'd blow my cheeks up with air, and their fingers would slip.

Jennifer and I still met on Saturdays. We always walked to the magic circle. Sometimes it was snowing and sometimes it was slushy, but Jennifer always brought her wagon. Sometimes now we talked about nonwitch stuff. Jennifer knew a lot about a lot of things. Partly her being a witch and partly her reading so much. For example, one week my apprentice food was five uncooked spaghettis every day. She told me all about how spaghetti was really Chinese but Marco Polo brought it home to Italy where it was a real success. She told me about how it was manufactured and how much it cost to buy stock in some famous macaroni company on the New York Stock Exchange.

We were really working on the flying ointment. Some of the ingredients were going to take a long time to collect, so Jennifer decided that we had to start immediately. For example, she decided that we needed about two teaspoonfuls of fingernail parings—one teaspoon from each of us. It takes a lot of parings to fill a spoon. I had to quit biting my nails, which made my mother the happiest woman in the whole U.S. of A. I figured that toenails and fingernails were all pretty much the same, so I also saved toenail cuttings. I saved them all in an old BAND AID box, which I kept in my underwear drawer along with the key and Jennifer's notes. I wore the key only on Saturdays.

Jennifer said that Christmas was a dangerous time of year for witches because everyone acted happy and tried to be good; Christmas week required special precautions. She said that instead of eating a special food, we were to give up a special food, and it wouldn't count to give up any old food. It had to be a food you especially loved. I thought a long time, trying to make up my mind whether to give up candy or give up cake. I loved candy more, and so to prove myself absolutely honest, I said to Jennifer, 'I'll give up candy.'

Jennifer said, 'I'll give up watermelon.'

'For how long?' I asked.

'Until New Year's Day, January the 1st, at 7.00 P.M. o'clock of the evening,' she answered.

'I know P.M. is the evening, Jennifer,' I answered.

'Agreed?' she asked.

'I even know that A.M. is of the morning, Jennifer,' I answered.

'Agreed?' she asked.

'I even know that New Year's Day is January the 1st, Jennifer.' I was getting tired of her telling me everything twice. Like New Year's Day and January the 1st; like P.M. and of the evening. But she still wouldn't argue.

'Agreed?' she asked.

'Agreed,' I answered.

Then we hooked our fingers together and marched around the magic circle. Jennifer said that our chants must be especially powerful this time. We had to be careful to face inward in the circle so that our heels and not our toes made prints in the outer rim of the circle. Like when your mother makes a pie crust, and she presses the crust around the rim of the pan with a fork. Always in the same direction.

As we marched around, toes always pointing inwards, Jennifer kept repeating this chant:

> 'Hecate, Hecate, Dock,
> Around this circle we walk.
> Within one hour make candy sour
> And melon hard as a rock.'

Then she carefully stepped out of the magic circle and motioned for me to do the same. I did. She sat down on the park bench closest to the circle and removed her boots. She motioned for me to do the same. I did. She put her socks inside her shoes, which were inside her boots, and stood up. She motioned for me to do the same. I did. She started walking towards the magic circle. She motioned for me to do the same. I didn't. My feet were frozen. She turned around and motioned for me again. She looked cross. I followed.

We walked around the magic circle again making certain that we never stepped out of the footprints we made the first time. As we walked around, we both chanted:

> 'Hecate, Hecate, Dock,
> Around this circle we walk.
> Within one hour make candy sour
> And melon hard as a rock.'

Then we both stepped out of the circle being careful to not make any new footprints. Jennifer walked, but I ran. My feet were numb from the cold. We dried our feet with our socks and put on our shoes without socks, then put on our boots. I stuffed my socks into my jacket pocket, and Jennifer dumped hers into the wagon. We walked back and looked at the beautiful pattern we had made in the snow. Our circle looked extra magical then.

Jennifer reached down and dug the snow out of two of the footprints. It was pressed down and a little bit dirty. She rolled two snowballs and gave one to me.

'We'll need this for our flying ointment,' she said. 'Save it in your deep freezer.'

Jennifer dumped her snowball into her wagon. I held mine in my hands. I had forgotten my mittens. My hands were freezing; my feet were freezing. I took my socks out of my pocket and put them on my hands. That helped a little.

Then Jennifer said, 'On New Year's Day at 7.00 P.M. o'clock of the evening, you'll find a note pinned to the tree. Read the note. Do as it says. No F.F. until then. The note will tell when we'll meet again.'

'F.F.?' I asked.

'Forbidden Food,' she answered.

Without another word she tilted her head upwards, her eyes upwards, and started home. I didn't dare wish her a Merry Christmas. That would not have been witching.

I walked home. Rather fast. I thought as I walked that I really loved watermelon, too. Maybe I should have made that my F.F. instead of candy. I was almost at our apartment door before I realized that I had never, absolutely never, heard of *anyone* having watermelon for Christmas. Maybe they did in Australia or New Zealand where they were below the equator and where everything was upside down, but I never heard of watermelon at Christmas in the whole U.S. of A.

That week we had staying guests: Aunt Drusilla and Uncle Frank. They are really my father's aunt and uncle, which makes them my great-aunt and great-uncle. The only thing great about them I could see was their ages. Together they were 133 years old. They had never had any children, and they thought that kids were pets who talked. I never sat near them. If I did, they would stroke my hair and pat my arm all the time. They were great cheek-pinchers. They would smile at me and say, 'Does our Lizzie want an ice cream?' Everything they said turned out to be a question. Instead of 'Good morning' they always said, 'Isn't it a good morning?' They said things like, 'My, isn't she a handsome girlie?' Something else about them was that they had the most peculiar food habits I have ever seen.

They ate something called Health Foods, which they brought with them in big cardboard boxes from a special Health Food store in Manhattan. They had boxes called *Lion's Milk* and all kinds of seeds and several kinds of honey and strange juices like sauerkraut juice and celery syrup. My mother would put our supper on the table and then spread out all these crazy seeds and stuff for the Greats. You can imagine how my mother looked when they first came and my father carried in all that stuff. She waited until they were in the bedroom unpacking their clothes. Then she came over to me. She bent to my ear and said in a low, slow voice, 'If – you – dare – to – ask – for – one – crazy – food – this – week – I'm – moving – into – a – hotel – and – no – one – will – hear – from – me – until – after – the – 4th – of – July.'

So I had been relieved when Jennifer said that for my apprenticeship this week, I had to give up something special instead of eat something special.

I walked in with my socks on my hands, dripping this dirty snowball across the rug, trying to get to the freezer.

The Greats spotted me. Great-aunt Drusilla got up from the couch and said, 'What are we doing, dearie?'

I knew that I had time to think of an answer because Great-uncle Frank always repeated what Great-aunt Drusilla said. She always returned the courtesy; she repeated what he said.

Great-uncle Frank did not disappoint me; he asked, 'What are we doing, dearie?'

I said, 'Putting this in the freezer.'

Great-uncle Frank said, 'And why are we doing that?'

Great-aunt Drusilla said, 'And why are we doing that?'

I said, 'To keep it frozen.'

Great-aunt Drusilla said, 'And why are we keeping it frozen?'

Great-uncle Frank said, 'And why are we keeping it frozen?'

I said, 'For an experiment.'

G.A. Drusilla said, 'And is this for school, sweetie?'

G.U. Frank said, 'And is this for school, sweetie?'

I said, 'Science class.'

G.A. Drusilla said, 'Oh?'

G.U. Frank said, 'Oh?'

I said, 'Yes?' and marched to the freezer. The puddle on the living room rug wasn't too big.

My mother came out of the bedroom just as I was closing the freezer. She took only a quick look at me and only a quick look at the puddle and said, 'Take off those boots.' I sat down on a kitchen chair and did. I forgot that my socks were on my hands and not on my feet. My mother noticed. When I had removed only the left shoe, she didn't quite believe that I had actually put on shoes and boots without socks. She waited until I took off the right shoe, too, to make sure. Then she said, 'Do you really believe that you're not going to catch a cold all winter because of that onion business weeks ago?'

I shook my head, 'Yes.'

She said, 'Have you ever thought that most people wear their socks on their feet, not on their hands?'

I shook my head, 'Yes.'

She said, 'Will you repeat after me : socks are for feet; mittens are for hands.'

I said, 'Socks are for feet; mittens are for hands.'

She said, 'Say it again.'

I said, 'Socks are for feet; mittens are for hands.'

She said, 'Now please tell me, where are your mittens?'

I said, 'In my sock drawer.'

She threw up her hands, 'Just get those socks off your hands and set the table.'

As usual the Greats helped me set the table. They were very accurate about where the fork and knife went. Everything about food except how it tasted interested them. They cared about the vitamins it had in it and about what order it was served in and how fast it was eaten. They ate very slowly. They believed in chewing. 'Proper mastication is essential to proper digestion,' they said. Each said it for each meal. That makes two Greats times three meals a day or six times a day I heard it. On the third day, I looked up *mastication*. It means *chewing*. I thought that after they left, I'd send their slogan in for a toothpaste commercial.

The Greats nibbled their seeds and sipped their sauerkraut juice. I couldn't decide whether they loved to eat or hated to eat. Maybe they ate slowly so that the meal wouldn't end. Maybe they ate slowly because everything tasted so bad that they had to eat slowly to get it down.

I began to snitch samples of all their foods. I wrapped them in waxed paper and pinned a label on them. After all, I figured, not many apprentice witches could get Lion's Milk for their flying ointment. Even in Africa where there are plenty of witches called witch doctors and plenty of lions, not many witches get lion's milk. I thought it would be a useful ingredient; lions can leap great distances. Lion's Milk, I thought, could be lift-off juice. Except that Lion's Milk was a powder. I kept all these little packages in my underwear drawer near the key and the notes and the fingernails. My underwear drawer was getting lumpy.

On New Year's Eve my mother and father went to a party. It was the first party they had gone to in a long time. My mother was anxious to go, but she worried about it for a week. My mother worried about manners. Since the Greats were our house guests, she thought that it wouldn't be polite to go to the party without them. Since she didn't know the hostess very well, she didn't want to ask her to ask the Greats. She thought that it would be impolite to not go to the party after she had already said yes.

One night my mother was telling her politeness worries to my father. She was saying, 'Maybe I should tell them that this invitation came at the very last minute and that it is important to your work to accept, and then ask them to please help out in this *emergency*.'

The reason I know all this is because I had to sleep on a cot in their room while the Greats were visiting. My father was dozing. I guess when he heard *emergency*, he became wide awake.

'Emergency!' he said.

'Sh, sh, sh,' my mother said.

'What is this? A *quiet* emergency?' my father asked.

'No, no, no,' my mother answered. 'I just thought that if we tell Aunt Drusilla and Uncle Frank that this *emergency* invitation came, and we just *have* to accept, they won't mind sitting with Elizabeth on New Year's Eve.'

'Are you still worrying about that?' my father asked. 'Why don't you tell them the truth?'

'The truth! The truth!' my mother answered. 'How can I tell them the truth?'

'Is the truth so bad?' my father asked. I could tell he was sleepy. 'Maybe I don't understand the facts. What *is* the truth?'

'Simply that we were invited and they weren't,' my mother answered.

My father gave a tiny laugh and said, 'Sounds terrible. I'll handle it in the morning.'

I started to laugh, too, but quickly buried my head in my pillow. My mother realized for the first time that I was awake.

'Elizabeth,' she called.

I didn't answer.

'Elizabeth,' she called. 'I know you're awake, and if you utter one word of this to your aunt and uncle, you'll sleep in the bath tub for the rest of their visit.' I didn't utter a sound.

My father 'handled' it in the morning. He simply told his aunt and uncle that he and mother would be going out on New Year's Eve.

Great-aunt Drusilla said, 'Isn't it wonderful to be young and to go out to parties?'

Great-uncle Frank said, 'Isn't it wonderful to be young and to go out to parties?'

I don't know why they said that Mom and Dad were young. I know for a fact that each was well over twice my age.

Father then said, 'I know you'll enjoy staying with Elizabeth.'

Great-uncle Frank said, 'Will we be baby-sitters?'

Great-aunt Drusilla said, 'Will we be baby-sitters?'

Father said, 'Yes.'

Great-aunt Drusilla said, 'Isn't that wonderful, Frankie?'

Great-uncle Frank said, 'Isn't that wonderful Frankie ... er ... ah ... I mean, Drusie?'

They could hardly wait for Mom and Dad to go to the

party. My parents got all dressed up. I could tell that my mother was excited about going out. She combed her hair front and back. She usually didn't check the back of her hair by holding up a small mirror in front of the big mirror, but she did for New Year's Eve. Actually, they didn't look too old when they were all dressed up; they just looked mature.

I have never been so well baby-sat. The Greats laid out my pyjamas and folded down the covers of my cot. They filled the bathtub for me and checked the temperature of the water. Great-uncle Frank called it 'drawing my bath'. Great-aunt Drusilla even put the toothpaste on my toothbrush for me. After I got to bed, both of them came into the bedroom every half hour to check me. It was almost impossible to go to sleep. They kept covering me. Every part of me was covered except those parts I needed for breathing.

New Year's Day was cloudy and cold. My father slept through the first breakfast of the new year. My mother got up and kept smiling and yawning and thanking the Greats for baby-sitting. At five minutes before 7.00 P.M. I went to the Jennifer tree. I carried a flashlight; it was very dark out. It was also very cold. I got to the tree, and there was the note in Jennifer's own writing. It said:

Near the roots
You'll find a treasure
Eat it up
At your pleasure
But save the seeds

Everyone
They'll be used
Before we're done.

Saturday. Library.
Half after 2:00 P.M. o'clock
of the afternoon

I bent down towards the roots of the tree. The flashlight shone on something small and round. I picked it up. It was the roundest, cutest watermelon I had ever seen in my whole, entire life. I carried it home, cradled it in my arms like a baby. When I walked into the living room, I put it in the middle of the floor and asked, 'Watermelon, anyone?'

Everyone asked the same question at the same time, 'Where did you get that?' I answered that I found it under a tree. I held it high over my head and led the parade to the kitchen. Even the Greats dug in and enjoyed it.

'Save the seeds!' I yelled.

Everyone was so busy eating, no one even asked me why.

7

The last Saturday of our winter vacation was a lazy day. I got up late and didn't do much until just before 2.00 P.M. except watch Great-aunt Drusilla and Great-uncle Frank pack for their trip home. They weren't leaving until after supper, but they began packing after breakfast. I think they would have stayed longer, but they were almost out of Health Foods. They wanted to get back to Manhattan for a fresh supply.

My mother breathed a sigh of relief when I told her that I was going to the library. I think she was exhausted from vacuuming; she had to vacuum three times a day because the Greats scattered so many seeds after each meal. I suggested to my mother that we get a parakeet instead of vacuuming. She hit me.

When I got to the library, I saw Jennifer's wagon outside the reference room. Jennifer was reading the encylopedia, volume Vase–Zygote. I had not seen her for over a week. I was anxious to find out how she had spent her vacation. When she saw me walking in she looked up and whispered, 'Did you bring anything to eat?'

'Some nuts,' I answered.

'What kind?' she asked.

'Brazil nuts,' I answered.

'Hard to crack,' she said. She got up from the table and checked out her books. We piled our reading supply into

Jennifer's wagon. Then we started towards the park. As we walked, we took turns pulling the wagon. I said, 'Thanks for the watermelon. Where did you get it this time of year.'

'Same place you did,' she answered.

'But I just picked it off the ground,' I said, and she answered, 'That's where they grow.' She gave me a sideways look and then marched on with her chin up, eyes up towards the sky. She never looked down as we walked. Even when we were going up and down curbs. She never fell or bumped into anything. Sometimes in school, I would see her walking down the hall reading a book. She could turn corners in the corridor, and she could open doors while she was still reading her book. She never tripped or fell. Reading and walking were her two best subjects, you might say.

Our magic circle was a mess. It was all grey and slushy and full of crumbs someone had thrown out for the squirrels and the birds. Jennifer looked at it and said, 'Isn't it beautiful?' I looked at it and shrugged my shoulders. We hooked our fingers together and marched around as we always did to start. Then we sat down on the bench and began cracking and eating the Brazil nuts. Jennifer reached into her wagon and brought out a big box of salt . . . as if she had been certain that I would bring nuts or something that needed salt. Before salting each nut she licked it a little so that the salt would stick.

As we were eating our nuts, Cynthia and Dolores walked through the park. They were going ice skating. Both of them had ice skates over their shoulders. Dolores was sensibly dressed. She had on ski pants, a jacket, mittens, boots, stocking cap, and earmuffs. That was just the top layer. That was all I could see. That was what my mother called sensibly dressed. Cynthia was *in*-sensibly dressed. She had on one of those short skirts that flare out when you twirl, if you know how to twirl on ice. I hoped she was cold.

I had been an apprentice for a couple of months now. I thought that if I could just make Cynthia trip and fall down, all my apprenticeship would be worth it. As they walked past me, I followed them silently with my eyes and chanted to myself, 'Trip and fall. Trip and fall. Trip and fall. Trip and fall.' As they passed, Cynthia tripped over the handle of Jennifer's wagon. Since she tripped but did not fall, I felt like a one hundred per cent successful *half* witch.

After we finished eating all the nuts, we got down to business. Jennifer asked if I had eaten any F.F. before New Year's Day. I replied that I was insulted that she should even ask. Then I described the seeds and the Lion's Milk I had collected from the Greats. She looked pleased. I told her about how they always said everything as if it were a question. She looked pleased, so I imitated how Great-aunt Drusilla and Great-uncle Frank always repeated what each other said. For a minute I thought Jennifer was going to laugh. She didn't; she looked pleased, though.

Next Jennifer surprised me. She gave me a promotion. I was graduated from apprentice witch to journeyman witch. Now I was no longer to eat special foods. Instead, I was to take very careful precautions. She went over these precautions one by one. She called them taboos.

Taboo 1 : Never lie on a pillow when I sleep.

Taboo 2 : Never cut my hair. (I saw some problems there. I was already playing hide and seek through my fringe. My mother kept saying that she would cut it as soon as she had a minute free from vacuuming.)

Taboo 3 : Never eat after 7.30 P.M. o'clock of the evening.

Taboo 4 : Never make a call on the telephone. I

asked Jennifer if I had permission to answer the phone if someone called me. Jennifer said, 'Of course.' She continued with the list.

Taboo 5 : Never wear shoes in the house on Sundays.

Taboo 6 : Never use red ink.

Taboo 7 : Never light a match.

Taboo 8 : Never touch straight pins or needles.

Taboo 9 : Never dance at a wedding.

Taboo 10 : Never get into bed without walking around it three times. (Another problem : my bed was in a corner pushed against the wall. Either I would have to convince my mother to change my room around, or I'd have to pull it out at night.)

Taboo 11 : Never walk on the same side of the street as a hospital.

Taboo 12 : Never sing before breakfast.

Taboo 13 : Never cry before supper.

Some of these taboos seemed pretty hard. I told Jennifer that I didn't think some of them made any sense. She told me that if I were looking for things to make sense, perhaps I wasn't yet ready for promotion. I asked Jennifer if she always obeyed the taboos. She said that she always did – except that now she was allowed to light matches. I remembered that she had had to light a candle when I first became her apprentice. I was convinced that I could, I would, obey. I asked Jennifer for a list of the taboos so that I wouldn't disobey by mistake. She said that witches don't rely on lists. The list might get lost and fall into the hands of some good person and that would mean trouble for witches all over. She said that I must memorize the list before school started the next day. She was afraid that back at school my mind would be all cluttered up with school stuff. Right then I had to learn them all; Jennifer checked me. She stood up and said to me, 'You have reached the end of your apprenticeship. You are now a journeyman witch.'

I was pleased. I asked, 'What comes next?'

'A master witch,' she answered.

'Are you a master?' I asked.

'Of course,' she replied. 'Only masters can train new witches.'

'What can a journeyman witch do?' I asked.

'You can cast short spells. Like making people trip.'

I smiled happily. I had already done that; I began to feel full of electricity. 'When will I become a master witch?' I asked.

'After we've successfully made the ointment and successfully used it,' she answered.

I was so happy that I almost flew up to our apartment. I stopped short at the door and took off my shoes. I wanted to practice for Sundays.

School is very dull in January and February. No holidays, nothing to do but learn until Washington's birthday on February 22nd. Sometimes it snowed and sometimes it slushed, but we always met on Saturdays. I saved up everything that happened to me during the week to tell Jennifer. She seemed to enjoy all the details of life in the apartment house. She told me things, too. Not things about her other life, though. She talked about her *interests*. She was interested in weaving. She wanted to weave cloth so that it could have a pattern in it. The pattern would be seen only if the cloth was held in a special way. And the pattern she wanted to weave in was people's names ... people she didn't like and sometimes people she liked. Then, if she folded the cloth, the person whose name was almost-invisibly-woven would double over with cramps; if she snipped a few of the pattern threads, the person whose name was almost-invisibly-woven would get a slight cut. She let me imagine what other things could happen to the cloth. The people she liked whose names were almost-invisibly-woven would stay smooth and clean and well aired. Jennifer was also interested in cryptography. We tried to talk in a couple of the codes she made up, but it took awfully long to say anything, and, after all, we had only our Saturdays together.

One Saturday in February we didn't meet. I'll tell about that one now.

Cynthia had a birthday party, and she invited me. I was amazed when I got the invitation. It came in the mail. *R.S.V.P.* was printed at the bottom. My mother said that *R.S.V.P.* meant that I had to let her know if I would come or not. I told my mother that I guessed I couldn't make it. She asked me why not. I told her that I was busy on Saturday.

'Doing what?' she asked.

'Going to the library,' I answered.

'Can't you do that work some other time?' she asked. At this point I have to admit that I had never yet told my mother about Jennifer. She thought that I went to the library every Saturday to do schoolwork. At first I didn't tell her because she didn't ask. Later I didn't tell her because I didn't want to. Because Jennifer was a witch. And my mother always liked me to have cousins and proper friends. Besides, witchcraft is a private affair.

My mother was worried about what she called my 'social development'. That means that she thought I should make some friends.

I had heard my mother and father discussing me one night when they thought that I was asleep. My mother told my father that she didn't think it was *normal* for me to be happy without friends. My father told her that a usual body temperature was 98·6 degrees, but some people were healthy with a body temperature of only 98·4 degrees. That was *normal* for them. 'So who's to say exactly what *normal* is?' my father said. My mother seemed to understand. For a while after this, she didn't bother me about my 'social development'. Until Cynthia's invitation came. Immediately, my mother began believing again that *normal* must be 98·6 degrees.

'Go to the library after school on weekdays and finish up your work. Then you'll be able to go to the party. I think it's very nice of Cynthia to invite you.'

'Her mother made her do it,' I said.

'That's a mean thing to say. It shows you don't think much of Cynthia, and it shows that you think even less of yourself.' She paused a minute, pointed a finger at me and said, 'You're going. Call Cynthia now.' With that, she took the receiver from the telephone and held it out for me. How could I tell my mother that I wouldn't go and also tell her that I wouldn't use the phone? I hadn't yet broken a single taboo. I didn't want anything as foolish as Cynthia's party to make me break one.

I thought fast; I talked fast. 'I won't bother to telephone. I'll run upstairs with my message.'

'That's the spirit,' my mother answered.

I went upstairs, knocked on Cynthia's door and R.S.V.P.'d, 'Yes.'

Cynthia said that she was delighted that I could come and that she was sorry she couldn't invite me in right then, but she was busy. Her good manners didn't impress me. They just told me that her mother was within hearing distance. Her good manners always got me mad.

Now I was faced with a real problem: letting Jennifer know that I couldn't meet her on Saturday. I wrote her a note explaining the situation. I pinned it to the Jennifer tree on my way to school the next morning. When school was dismissed at lunch, I checked the tree and saw that she had put a note in its place. Jennifer had answered:

Give Heed !!

While at the party
Be on awaref.
Do not eat cake
Or play musical chairf.

After I had told Cynthia 'yes' and after I had received this permission from Jennifer, I was glad that I was going to the party. I enjoyed getting mad at Cynthia. I also thought that it would be fun to tell Jennifer all about how ordinary girls act at a party; normal girls who had a temperature of 98·4 degrees.

From the first moment I awakened on the Saturday of the party, things did not go well. Not at all. In the first place it was a butterscotch day; I was never in a good mood on butterscotch days. There was a candy factory in our town. On different days they made different flavours. In our part of town, we breathed flavoured air. Orange was pleasant; cherry and lime were hardly noticeable; mint was delicious (I could pretend that I was smoking a menthol cigarette). But butterscotch was a hard flavour to breathe.

In the second place, my mother looked at my hair and decided that I couldn't go to the party without a trim. Especially my bangs. She said something about my head looking like a pot of spaghetti that had boiled over. She ran to get the scissors. I ran to get my bathing cap.

'Get that thing off your head,' she said. 'All I want to do is trim your bangs.'

'I want them to grow out. Please,' I answered.

'How can you possibly look neat for the party?' she asked.

'I'll shampoo it and pin it back,' I answered. 'After all, it is my hair.'

'I never doubt that it's yours,' my mother said, 'but I sometimes doubt that it's hair. Okay, go wash it.'

I worked hard on the shampoo job, and I used about fifty thousand bobby pins to hold it back. If someone had held a magnet anywhere near my head, I feel certain that it would have lifted me five feet off the floor.

My party dress was also a problem; it was two years old. I always grew, but every year I grew less than most people. If I had grown a great deal, my mother would have bought me a new dress, but everything always *almost* fitted, and so we managed to get another year's wear out of it. That was what had happened with the Pilgrim costume, too. I was very uncomfortable. With my hair pinned back tight and my dress so tight, I felt as if I wouldn't be able to move unless someone pulled my arms and legs with strings the way you pull a marionette. I was in no party mood.

My mother wrapped the gift she had gotten for Cynthia. Two days before, she had asked me what I thought Cynthia would like; I had answered, 'A pet boa constrictor.' My mother didn't think that was very funny. She bought her a pair of stretch gloves, since we didn't know her size.

I went up to Cynthia's apartment and rang the bell. When she opened the door and greeted me, all I could see was pink. She was wearing a pink dress. Pink balloons were hanging from the ceiling; the table was set with pink paper cups and pink paper dishes. In the middle of the table was a pinkly frosted cake.

I limped in. I had planned a limp right after Jennifer's note. I needed an excuse to not play musical chairs, so I invented a sore leg. Most of the girls were late for the party. All were in the fifth grade at William McKinley Elementary School, but I hadn't been to a party with them before. They were either surprised to see me there or else they didn't recognize me with my hair pinned back. They would look over at me and say 'Hi', then look again and say 'Oh, hi, I didn't recognize you at first.' I wasn't being a great social success at the party. The party wasn't being a great social success with me.

Instead of turning a record player or radio on and off for musical chairs, Cynthia played the piano. I hoped the neighbours on the fifth floor who lived under her would call up and complain about the noise. They didn't. Cynthia probably had them enchanted. To what Cynthia could do, there was no end; to what I, Elizabeth, the journeyman witch, could do, there was no start.

I couldn't play pin the tail on the donkey (there was a pink donkey and pink tails, imagine!) because I could not touch pins: Taboo Number 8. I couldn't play musical chairs; I couldn't eat cake: Jennifer's warning. I was

so miserable about my hair and musical chairs and my dress that I tried hard to accidentally forget the taboos. I tried to make a slight mistake that couldn't possibly be my fault; but the harder I tried, the harder it was to forget that I was a journeyman witch. Then I thought that, perhaps, this party was one of the torture trials I had read about in the *Black Book*. So I decided instead to enjoy being odd. And I did.

After pin the tail and musical chairs, everyone played treasure hunt. The treasure was the prize. I found the treasure with no trouble at all. As soon as the treasure hunt was announced, I walked straight to it. It was under the sofa pillow. I had sat on it during musical chairs and pin the tail. I had been too polite to mention the lump in the sofa. All the girls said, 'Oh, how did you?' I just shrugged my shoulders and gave them a Jennifer-type look. The treasure was a little box of chocolates. Squashed chocolates.

The next and last game was dropping clothes pins into a milk bottle. I got nine in. I won. Sometimes being short was nice. My prize was a package of hair ribbons. Four of them were pink. When I opened it and saw what it was, I said, 'Well, it looks as if I have this prize all tied up.' Everyone looked at me and smiled. I didn't smile back.

Then we all sat at the pinkly-pinkly table. Maria and Helen sat on either side of me and didn't seem to mind sitting there at all. First, Cynthia opened her presents. She said, 'Oh, how lovely!' every single time. It was disgusting. Before she opened each gift she held it up and said, 'I wonder who this is from?' She was just asking; she didn't want an answer. I answered. I said, 'Maria,' or 'Dolores,' or whoever the correct person was. I had been the first one at the party, and it was easy to remember who brought what. But when they asked, 'Elizabeth, how do you do it?' I gave them another Jennifer-type look.

Finally, Cynthia's mother lit the candles on the cake and everyone sang 'Happy Birthday to You'. I didn't sing. I know everyone wondered why. They didn't ask. I didn't explain. I couldn't explain. I couldn't tell them that I was enjoying being different.

It was even no trouble to not eat cake. No trouble at all.

Cynthia stood by the door and said, 'Good-bye and thank you for coming' to everyone. She said it to me, too, but she didn't mean it. She said it because her mother was standing there, behind her back. That's the only reason. I know that's the only reason because as she said it, she screwed up her face and stuck out her tongue.

I said, 'Good-bye, and thank you for inviting me.' I said it loud enough for her mother to hear. Then I stepped on Cynthia's foot as hard as I could. With my 'sore' leg. Just once. I left without looking back. I could bet that my normal temperature was not 98.4 degrees.

When I got back to our apartment, my mother asked, 'Did you thank for the party?'

I answered, 'Of course.' The whole day had changed. The wind had changed and the air wasn't butterscotch. It was freshly baked bread. There was also a bread factory in our town.

8 I shared with Jennifer my prizes from the party. I told her all about how pink everything was, and I told her how I won the treasure, and I told her about calling out the names on the gifts. I described these tricks with pride. Jennifer allowed me to finish before she made me feel dumb, 'You must be careful never to show your witchcraft in public. Don't be tempted into showing off.'

'But, Jennifer,' I said, 'you can hardly call those tricks *witchcraft*. I just memorized those gifts, and I happened to accidentally sit on the treasure.'

Jennifer looked serious. She said, 'Why do you think it was so easy to memorize those names?'

'Because I was the first one at the party?' I answered.

'Why do you think you were the first one at the party?' she asked.

'Because my mother sent me up there early?' I answered.

Jennifer paused a minute to let me think. Then she said, 'Why do you think you sat on the treasure?'

'Because you said that I couldn't play musical chairs?'

'Why do you think I said you couldn't play musical chairs?' she asked.

'Because ... because ... because I don't know,' I answered.

She said no more about the party, so I said no more. I felt disappointed because I had saved up much more gossip. Watching normal girls and collecting things to tell her about how they acted had helped me during the party. I couldn't understand why Jennifer didn't want to hear about normal girls.

We returned to business. We began as usual by hooking our fingers together and marching around the magic circle. It took me a little while to want to talk witch talk; I was still in a party mood. But the magic of our circle worked. We discussed our plans for the flying ointment.

I had completed my first responsibility. I had listed all the ingredients. Most of the recipes needed plants like foxglove, cowbane, and my very favourite, deadly nightshade. I had felt certain that every witch would put witch hazel on the list; not one did. Jennifer called the items from these famous recipes, *general ingredients*. Everyone needed the general ingredients, but everyone also needed special ingredients. Everyone could use the same general parts, but each witch must use some particular things that were different from all the other witches' things. That's why we had our particular fingernails and our particular snowball footprints.

The way we divided the work was that Jennifer learned the chants and got the general stuff. I got my own special stuff, some of hers, the charcoal for the fire, and the three-pound can of lard. We needed the lard as a base for the ointment so that it would really stick. We had thought about using Vaseline, but we decided that it would be hard to get three pounds of Vaseline. When I took the lard, I planned to tell my mother that it was for the needy. I was the needy.

I was worried about getting foxglove, cowbane, and deadly nightshade. Jennifer told me not to worry. 'Where will you get them?' I asked.

'From my father.'

I was amazed. 'Is your father a wizard?'

'Some people say that he is a plant wizard,' she muttered.

'Honest?' I said. 'A real wizard!'

'I said *plant* wizard,' she answered.

'Oh, Jennifer,' I gasped. 'How wonderful! My father is only a commuter.'

Then Jennifer said, 'Maybe we should make a flying potion instead.'

'What's the difference between a flying ointment and a flying potion?' I inquired.

'You drink a potion; it works from the inside. You salve a flying ointment all over yourself; it works from the outside.'

'Drink it?' I asked.

'Yes. There's a plant that grows in South America called *ayahuasco*. We could use that. Maybe some jungle witch could fly it here.'

'Drink it?' I squealed.

'Yes,' she repeated.

'I vote for the ointment.'

Jennifer sighed, 'It does seem a shame to waste all of our research. We'll have all our general ingredients ready for spring vacation.' I somehow knew that Jennifer was relieved that I voted for the ointment. I somehow knew that she mentioned the potion just to stop me from thinking about her father. I enjoyed knowing without letting her know that I knew.

The weather in March is a lot like me. Nice for one day and then nasty for two. In March I'm always waiting for warm days, and when they come, I wonder why I waited. My mother never admits that it can be warm in March. She always insists that I wear an undershirt and my heavy winter coat until May. She never has my heavy winter coat cleaned in March. She waits to clean it for summer storage. Neither my mother nor the weather can decide whether winter isn't quite over or whether winter is almost over. So I spend the warm days of March in my heavy, itchy, dirty winter coat. And in my undershirt. I spend the warm days of March uncomfortably. But I wait for them.

When we met on Saturdays in March, Jennifer always brought Hilary Ezra with her. Hilary Ezra was our toad. Around New York most people don't have toads in March. Around New York most people don't have toads in March or watermelons in January. Jennifer was not most people. She came to the park the first Saturday in March and said, 'Today I brought the toad.' She held him out in her hand. He wasn't very big. For a minute I thought he was the plastic kind that you buy in kits. The kind that are stuck on a cardboard under one big plastic bubble. Sometimes they are glued on a card under separate little plastic bubbles, and the card says 'Farmyard Friends', or 'Dinosaurs – Great and Small'. The toad moved. I jumped. Jennifer closed her hand.

'Where did you get him?' I asked.

'Witches always have toads,' she answered. 'Toads are the first ingredient.' She paused a second, looked up towards the sky and said, 'What's the matter, didn't you ever read *Macbeth*?'

'Well, no,' I said, 'I've *heard* about *Macbeth*.'

'Every modern witch ought to read *Macbeth*,' Jennifer said. 'Those witches cooked up a wonderful brew. Not flying ointment brew. Trouble brew. And the first ingredient to go in was a toad.' Then Jennifer stared at me and recited:

> 'Round about the cauldron go:
> In the poison'd entrails throw.
> Toad, that under cold stone
> Days and nights has thirty one
> Swelter'd venom sleeping got,
> Boil thou first i' the charmèd pot.'

She stared at me the whole time she was reciting.

'Did Macbeth say that?'

'Of course not,' she scolded. 'Macbeth wasn't a witch. The witches say that as they stir their brew of trouble. Notice they boiled the toad first in the pot.'

'What are the witches' names in *Macbeth*?' I asked.

'First witch, second witch, third witch,' she answered, 'and Hecate, the queen of the witches is in it, too.'

'What kind of trouble was in the pot?' I asked.

'They gave him a warning,' she replied.

I thought a minute and said, 'It doesn't sound mean to warn someone. That doesn't sound like trouble. Sounds rather nice, as a matter of fact.'

'It wasn't nice,' Jennifer insisted. 'How can you be a witch and be good, too? The two just don't go together.'

'What did they warn him of?'

'The truth.'

I couldn't understand what could be so awful about

the truth. I had heard grown-ups talk about the *awful truth*, but I couldn't understand what they meant. So I asked, 'What's so bad about the truth?'

'They told him the truth in such a way that he got to feeling too sure of himself. He became careless and brought about his doom.'

'What did they tell him?' I asked.

'I won't tell. You have to read *Macbeth*. Every modern witch should. Those witches were wonderful.'

'Give me an example,' I begged. 'Please?'

'I'll give you an example of the *kind* of thing they did.' She thought a long minute before beginning. 'Suppose they said to you first, "Elizabeth, beware of ... beware of the toad. The toad will cause you pain." You think to yourself that you like the toad. Besides, you can't imagine how any toad with no sharp claws and no sharp teeth can cause you pain. But since the witches warned you – you will beware.'

'Yes,' I said, 'I would listen. They might mean that I'll get a wart and need to have it burned off.'

Jennifer nodded. 'Next they tell you that no animal born where rain can fall will harm you. Then you think to yourself ... toads are always born out of doors in a pond or a lake where rain can fall. So you don't have to worry much about the toad or about most animals.'

I silently agreed. Then Jennifer continued, 'Next they tell you that you'll have no pain until the home of the toad comes to you. You think ... how can a lake or a pond or a park come to me? So after the first warning, which you are perfectly willing to believe, you end up feeling pretty sure of yourself.'

'What's wrong with feeling pretty sure of yourself?' I asked.

'*Pretty* sure is okay. But *too* sure isn't okay. Imagine being so sure of yourself for a test that you never even open the book.'

'Oh, I'm never that sure.' I was watching the toad and wanting to pet him.

Jennifer was still concentrating on *Macbeth*. 'In *Macbeth*, Hecate says:

> "And you all know, security
> Is mortals' chiefest enemy." '

'Is man a mortal?' I asked.

'Of course,' Jennifer answered.

'Then, is that Hecate's way of saying the story of the tortoise and the hare? You know, that fable about the rabbit being so sure of winning the race that he wasn't even careful. He didn't try very hard to win.'

'Yes,' Jennifer explained. 'Except that they didn't make Macbeth sure of winning ... they made him sure he'd never lose.'

'Never lose what?' I demanded.

'His life,' she croaked. She looked at me hard. I swallowed hard.

'Jennifer,' I asked, 'what do you ever do besides read?'

She looked up at the sky and sighed and said very seriously, 'I think.' She continued looking up at the sky and added, 'Now do you absolutely understand about the witches' warning?'

'Macbeth's witches?' I asked.

'Any witches.'

I nodded. For just a minute the idea crossed my mind that Jennifer actually was warning me. Then I thought, 'Oh, well, how can a lovely little toad cause me pain?'

'May I hold him?' I asked.

'Of course.' She handed him to me.

'Jennifer, do witches ever name their toads?'

'Never,' she answered.

'I think we should,' I said.

'We shouldn't,' she said.

'I think we should call him *Hilary*. *Hilary* means cheerful. And he is bright-eyed and cheerful.'

'Witches don't name toads,' she said.

'Yep, Hilary is a fine name.'

'Witches don't name toads,' she repeated.

'*Hilary* means cheerful, and you are cheery, dearie,' I murmured. To the toad . . . not to Jennifer.

'He should be called *Ezra* if he's called anything at all,' she replied.

'Why Ezra?' I demanded.

'Because *Ezra* means *help* . . . and he'll help us make the flying ointment.'

'*Hilary* is better,' I insisted.

'Ezra,' she said.

'How about Hilary Ezra?' I asked.

'Agreed,' she answered.

I think I grew to love Hilary Ezra from that very second. Naming him was the first argument I ever won from Jennifer. For once *I* had convinced *her*. I thought.

We both loved Hilary Ezra. We always called him by his entire, complete name. We enjoyed catching insects for him to eat. We would bring a ruler to the park to see how far he would jump. We marked down the date. We would calculate his average jump for the day, his longest jump, his lifetime average, and his lifetime record. He was wonderful company for being such a dumb animal. He always wore a prize ribbon. Not first prize or second prize. One of my ribbons I had won at Cynthia's party.

Each of us tried to be kinder to Hilary Ezra than the other. We would argue about whose turn it was to pull him in the wagon. We placed an old window screen over the top of the wagon so that he couldn't jump out. He was not a grateful animal; he would try to jump out every time we took the screen away. It was easily true that each of us loved Hilary Ezra more than he loved us. Sometimes it almost seemed true that we loved

83

Hilary Ezra more than we loved each other. Hilary Ezra became the one thing that made me jealous of Jennifer. I admired the way she could read. I admired the way she could walk looking up at the sky. I admired the cool way she could ignore someone (even me) if she wanted to. I admired all these things. I always felt grateful when she shared her talents with me even if sharing them made her bossy. But I didn't feel grateful when she shared Hilary Ezra. I felt jealous because I wished that I could have him all the time. He had pretty eyes.

One day Jennifer brought Hilary Ezra to school in her pocket. It was warm that day and all the fifth grades were out on the playground playing kick ball. Hilary Ezra hopped out of Jennifer's pocket as she was guarding first base. The first person to notice was Tommy Schmidt. He had just kicked the ball and was on his way to first when he spotted Hilary Ezra. Everyone was yelling, 'Go, Tom, go. Run, Tom, run.' Tom did not go. Tom did not run. Tom stopped dead. Jennifer was looking up at the sky as usual. There was sudden quiet when Tom stopped. Jennifer reached down, picked up Hilary Ezra and put him back in her pocket. She buttoned her pocket closed. No one said a word. I smiled to myself. A very small smile. I couldn't let anyone knew that he was mine, too.

During March I was practising casting small journey-man witch spells. Sometimes I was successful. Here is a list of my successful spells:

1. Cynthia got sick and missed eight days of school. Miss Hazen made me take her homework to her every day. Besides, being only a journeyman witch, I couldn't make her terribly sick.
2. Miss Hazen didn't call for our arithmetic home-work the day I didn't do it.
3. It rained on the day of the class trip to the zoo. Everyone got sick. Two kids threw up. The bus

smelled awful from all the fumes and wet raincoats and all. The zoo didn't smell too good, either. I loved it.

4. Cynthia and Dolores had a fight. It lasted only a short while. I could still cast only short spells.

All in all, I was feeling very competent.

9

Spring vacation came. It was the middle of April. Jennifer and I had invested all of our Saturdays in witchcraft. We had invested bicycling time, movie time, roller-skating time, lounging-around-the-house-in-your-pyjamas time. Now we would see if it had been worth it.

We arranged to meet at the park at 7.00 A.M. o'clock of the morning. The first Monday of vacation. This meant that I had to be up at 6.30 A.M. o'clock of the morning. My mother heard me getting up and getting dressed. She came into my bedroom, glanced at the clock, said, 'I don't believe it,' and went back to bed. That saved my having to answer a lot of questions. I was nervous. I couldn't eat breakfast, partly because I wanted to be lighter for our flight.

I had written a list the night before. I checked off the items one by one. My fingernails, the watermelon seeds, the frozen snowball in an old milk carton, the foods the Greats had donated, the three pound can of lard, a spatula to get the lard out of the can, charcoal briquets and fluid to light them. I put everything into a large shopping bag from Bloomingdale's and carried it to the park.

Jennifer was already at the park when I got there. She had brought her big kettle somehow. Her whole wagon was filled with potted plants. With the screen over it, it looked like a tiny greenhouse on wheels. Maybe Jennifer had made two trips. Inside the kettle were the matches, her fingernails, and her snowball, now melted in an old herring jar. Her fingernails were saved in a match box. I could tell that she had just added to the supply because her fingernails were very short right then. Both of us had chanted for a windy day; we got one. It was warm, too. We decided that we had enough proper ingredients, the proper chants, and a good proper wind. We were ready to fly.

We knew exactly what we were supposed to do. We transferred the ingredients from the kettle to my Bloomingdale's shopping bag. Then we carried the kettle, the shopping bag and the wagon to near the centre of our magic circle where we placed them on the ground around the bottom of the water fountain. That done, we silently marched around the circle seven times. Each time around we went faster and faster. Then we went to the picnicking part of the park where there are barbecue grilles for people if they want to use them. I placed the charcoal on the grille and doused it with lighter fluid. Jennifer lit the match since she no longer had to obey Taboo 7. Together we lifted the huge cauldron to the top of the grille.

First we opened the can of lard and emptied it into the cauldron. Then Jennifer threw in the key that opened the can. We marched around and marched around the cauldron. We marched around and marched around. It seemed to take awful long for three pounds of lard to melt. We kept *silence* the whole time. The lard melted; then we added the other ingredients. She chanted, and I stirred after each addition. In went the deadly nightshade. 'Xilka, Xilka,' stir, stir. The snowballs; the lard steamed and cackled. 'Besa, Besa,' stir, stir. Next the foxglove. 'Xilka, Xilka,' stir, stir. Then the Lion's Milk. 'Besa, Besa,' stir, stir. The water-melon seeds. Chant and stir. The fingernails. Chant and stir. The food of the Greats. Chant and stir. All went into the pot. 'Xilka, Xilka, Besa, Besa,' stir, stir, stir.

Then Jennifer lifted the screen from the wagon and slowly withdrew Hilary Ezra from his home. She didn't look at me. She kept chanting as she reached up and dangled my lovely pet by one leg over the cauldron.

I gasped. I had forgotten that Hilary Ezra was a proper ingredient. Jennifer heard my gasp and saw the look of horror on my face. She gave me a cross look in return. We were not supposed to speak until we finished all our chanting. She was chanting and dangling my beautiful Hilary Ezra over the pot. I couldn't stand it one second longer. I yelled, 'STOP,' grabbed her wrist, and shook her hand until she dropped Hilary Ezra to the ground. He hopped away from us forever.

Jennifer said nothing. She picked up the empty lard can and walked to the magic circle water fountain. There she filled the can with water. She threw the water on the fire.

'What are you doing?' I asked.

'Putting out the fire,' she answered.

'I know that. I mean *why* are you doing it?'

'Ask what you mean,' she answered.

'All right,' I said. 'Then why are you doing it?'

'Because the spell is over. You'll never make a proper witch. You still want too many reasons *and* you are too sentimental.'

'And you, Jennifer, are too hard-hearted. You never even hesitated.'

'You are dismissed,' she said. She didn't even look up at me.

'You ...' I screamed, trying hard to think of something awful to call her. 'You ... you ... you ... you, JENNY!' I yelled and I walked away. I waited until I was out of the park before I began to cry.

I cried at first because I had lost Jennifer, Hilary Ezra, and the flying ointment. I cared in that order. I cried because I was angry with myself. Like flunking a test

because you didn't study and there's no excuse. I had flunked the flying ointment test. We had worked hard on it. As I got closer to home, I began to think about Hilary Ezra. Then I got mad at Jennifer. Not hurt feelings. Good mad feelings. That had been the first time I had ever disobeyed. I thought that Jennifer was mean. She was mean to Hilary Ezra, and she was mean to me. And I kept saying 'mean' to myself, but by the time I reached our apartment building, I realized something else. Jennifer was not being mean to Hilary Ezra. She wanted me to stop her from boiling him in oil. I remembered about the witches in *Macbeth*; the toad was supposed to be the first ingredient. She had told me that. She had purposely kept him until last. She had purposely dangled him over the pot so long. She always found a way to not get mad at herself but to get mad at me instead. I was sure if I hadn't stopped her, she would have stopped herself. By the time the elevator came, I was crying with rage.

When I walked into our apartment, my mother looked at me and said, 'What in the world happened to you?'

'I had a fight,' I answered.

'With whom?' she asked.

'Jennifer,' I replied.

'And who is Jennifer?' she asked.

'Some old witch,' I yelled and ran to my room and slammed the door.

10 If Jennifer hadn't told me that I was no longer a journeyman witch, I would have known anyway. The spell was over. The next morning, I came down with a cold. Not only did I have a virus, but my mother said that I probably got it from Cynthia. I had the same symptoms as she had had. I had picked up Cynthia's nasty germs. And they got ripe during vacation. I didn't even have a chance to miss school.

I cried a lot during that vacation. My mother thought it was mostly because I was sick and because my temperature really was not 98·4; it was higher. But, of course, it was only partly that. I got mad a lot, too. Like when I remembered that no one, absolutely no one, would notice when I snubbed Jennifer at school. No one at school knew that we even knew each other.

I was well enough to return to school on schedule. We began right where we left off, New Math and all. I didn't enjoy it too much. I still walked to school alone, of course. But for the first time since Halloween it seemed lonely. Thoughts of Jennifer had been good company. Looking for notes and leaving notes on the Jennifer tree had made each trip to school a tiny adventure. For a couple of days I tried walking to school by the sidewalk route. I didn't enjoy that any more. The men from the road department were shovelling the sand out of the gutters. In the winter they had thrown the sand out to keep the cars from slipping in the snow. Their shovels scraped along the sidewalk and gave me chills. My days as a witch were truly over.

I went back to walking through the woods. The ground was soft and moist; even the most sheltered snow had melted.

On Friday I searched the Jennifer tree during each of my four trips. I didn't find a note any time. On Saturday my mother started getting ready to go to the supermarket. I yelled, 'Wait a minute; I'm coming, too.'

She looked surprised and said, 'I thought you'd be going to the library as usual.'

'Oh,' I said, 'that project is finished.'

'Did you get an *A* on it?' my mother asked.

'Not exactly,' I answered.

'For all the work you did on that project, I thought you'd not only get an *A*, you'd get a medal.'

'Well,' I said, 'sometimes you work real hard on something and all you get for it is a stupid virus.'

'What does that mean?' my mother asked.

'Oh, I don't know,' I answered. I began to cry.

'It's that virus,' my mother said. 'You still haven't recovered. It must be the virus; you cried on and off that whole week you were in bed. I think it's one of the symptoms.'

Of course I was crying! Of course I had been crying! Jennifer had made the witches' warning come true. Hilary Ezra did cause me deep pain. Even though I couldn't explain the rest of that warning.

My mother was looking at me. She came over to me and put her hand under my chin and tilted my head upwards. She said very gently, 'Maybe you ought to stay in the apartment while Dad and I go to the store. Or maybe you'd like to invite Cynthia over.'

The thought of spending a morning with Cynthia while my spirits were so low made me stop crying. 'I'll stay. I'll stay alone,' I said. I said it loud, and I said it fast.

'I'll never understand why you don't like Cynthia,' my mother said. 'I think she's charming.'

'Mother,' I said, 'if you really want to know, I'll tell you why. Cynthia is a phony. I've known for a long time that she's a phony. And worse than that, she doesn't know she's a phony. She believes in Cynthia. She's a serious phony. And the only way I can stand her is to absolutely ignore her.'

'All right. All right,' my mother said. 'Stay here and don't let anyone in the apartment without finding out who it is. Peek through the peek hole.' She meant the eye-sized hole in the door that most apartments have. It has a tiny one-way mirror in it, and you can see out without the outsiders seeing in.

After Mom and Dad had been gone about twenty or twenty-five minutes, I was beginning to feel like the loneliest girl in the whole U.S. of A. I made myself a glass of chocolate milk using enough syrup for three normal glasses. I also made myself four peanut butter crackers. Then I walked out the living room door to our terrace.

The trees were coming! New green was all over ... green so new that it was kissing yellow. The windows of the greenhouse on THE ESTATE caught the sun and winked it back to me. As the shadows of the branches waved across the windows, the light seemed to blink on and off. A private kind of Morse code, I thought. I sat there staring at the roof of the greenhouse. It was pleasant on our terrace. I was happy that my mother had washed away the soot of winter and bought the porch furniture. The view from the terrace was far nicer than from anywhere else in the apartment. We hadn't really used the terrace since we moved in. In September we hadn't had porch furniture yet, and in October it had been so cold that we kept the terrace door locked. Then in April, right after Mom got it all ready, I got my virus.

THE ESTATE was the prettiest view we could see from our terrace. Looking in the other direction, we could see down Providence Street, but it was not nearly so peaceful. My eye kept wandering back to the green-house. The sun kept splashing on the windows. Blink. Blink. I decided that someday when I was rich and famous, I'd have a greenhouse. I'd have flowers all year round. I'd have fresh grown onions in winter, and I'd have water-melon in January.

WATERMELON IN JANUARY! Of course! TOADS IN MARCH! Of course! A place where no rain falls! Of course! The greenhouse was where Hilary Ezra had been born. And Jennifer's father was the plant wizard who grew the watermelon and the deadly night-shade. And Hilary Ezra's home did come to me that awful day in the park. Jennifer carried the greenhouse plants to the park in her wagon. There was a message in that Morse code of the windows. I was brilliant. I was a genius!

I was so pleased with my brilliance that I was angry that there was no one to tell about it. At least Jennifer would know I knew. I'd send her a special delivery letter in care of the Samellson Estate, and when she had to sign for the special delivery, she'd know that I had found her out. Or maybe I'd write her mysterious notes and leave them on the Jennifer tree ... but then I couldn't be cer-tain she'd get them. I'd call her on the phone except that I couldn't use the phone. No, of course I could use the phone. I had been dismissed. I'd get the phone book down and look up Mrs Samellson's number. Wouldn't Jennifer be surprised when she heard my voice. She'd wonder how I knew where to reach her.

I was growing more brilliant by the minute. Mrs Samellson was famous for her antiques. She would have a big three-legged kettle, and she would have a genuine Pilgrim dress. It had been easy for Jennifer to get my notes. Jennifer and I were neighbours! I was pacing the floor and eating salted cashew nuts, which I don't even like. I had to tell someone. I absolutely had to tell someone! I would cast a small spell. My mother would come home. I'd tell her! I'd test to see if I had any witchcraft left over. Then the doorbell rang. I pulled a chair over to the door so that I could look through the peek hole. I

didn't see anyone at first. Then I stood on tiptoes and looked way down at the floor. I saw a wagon. Jennifer's wagon! I jumped down from the chair and yanked the door wide open.

Jennifer walked into my house for the first time. Her eyes were up on the ceiling.

'Hi,' I said.

'Do you have anything to eat?' she answered. I stood with my mouth open. How could anyone have such terrible manners?

Then I answered, 'Oh, yes. What would you like? A raw egg? Or a raw onion? Perhaps you would like five uncooked spaghettis or some raw oatmeal? Which would you prefer?'

Jennifer looked at me and said, 'I really want just a drink of water.'

I laughed, 'But look at your empty wagon. You must, absolutely must, let me fill it up with trick or treat.'

Jennifer looked at me and smiled. First she smiled and then she laughed. Jennifer laughed. She really laughed and laughed and laughed. I also laughed. And then I laughed and laughed and laughed. For the first time we laughed together. We were laughing and playing together when my parents came home, and I introduced them to Jennifer. My mother smiled and said, 'Hi, can you both give me a hand unloading these groceries?' We both did. Jennifer seemed to know where everything went.

Now we laugh together a lot. We walk to school together, too. Sometimes I play at her house, the caretaker's house on THE ESTATE. Sometimes we visit Mrs Samellson who is even older than the Greats. She tells wonderful stories about her antiques. We don't even mind Cynthia to much. Neither of us is lonely any more. Sometimes we even play with Maria or Grace. But not too often. We don't have too much time to spare.

Neither of us pretends to be a witch any more. Now we mostly enjoy being what we really are ... just Jennifer and just me ... just good friends.